DANGER AT MELLIN COVE

In Cornwall, a dangerous world of passions and intrigue awaits Hedra St Neot. She agrees to help her brother, Kit, to run his Cornish inheritance: a wild and beautiful estate at Mellin Cove. But will she stay to help handsome fisherman, Jem Pentreath, protect the local community from her rogue uncle's band of cut-throat smugglers? Or will she finally agree to marry Sir Edward Tremaine, the rich mine owner who is besotted with her?

RENA GEORGE

DANGER AT MELLIN COVE

Complete and Unabridged

LINFORD
Leicester

First published in Great Britain in 2011

First Linford Edition
published 2012

British Library CIP Data

Duncan, Rena.
  Danger at Mellin Cove. - -
  (Linford romance library)
  1. Love stories.
  2. Large type books.
  I. Title II. Series
  823.9'2–dc23

  ISBN 978–1–4448–1109–4

Published by
F. A. Thorpe (Publishing)
Anstey, Leicestershire

Set by Words & Graphics Ltd.
Anstey, Leicestershire
Printed and bound in Great Britain by
T. J. International Ltd., Padstow, Cornwall

This book is printed on acid-free paper

1

The older rider slowed his mount to a trot, unsure of the rough terrain across the Cornish moors at night, but Hedra urged him on, gasping as the wind snatched at her words.

'Please, Dr Roskilly . . . oh, please,' she pleaded. 'We must hurry!'

Her sister-in-law's anguished cries of pain still rang in her head.

If only her father and brothers had not ridden off to Truro, then she and Rachel would not be facing this alone. But then no one knew the child would arrive so early.

The wind whipped past her galloping horse as Hedra glanced back, praying the elderly doctor was keeping up with her. She bit her lip, cursing her earlier encounter on the road that had cost her so much precious time.

The first flakes of snow were driving

in their faces as they approached the village and Hedra's heart quickened as she glimpsed the familiar dark shapes of the cottage roofs. Soon the low stone dwellings where the mining families lived would be behind them, and they would be racing on, taking the left fork in the road that swung towards the ocean — and home.

She strained for the first sounds of waves crashing into the shingle of St Neot's Cove. But despite her urgency, she couldn't resist looking back to the spot where, only an hour before, she might have met an unthinkable fate if the stranger had not stepped in to save her.

It had been an alarming encounter. At first she had thought her mare, Molly, had slipped, pitching her into the prickles of a gorse patch. Then she realised she was being dragged from her horse. A hand had clamped itself over her mouth, and an urgent voice instructed in her ear. 'Shush! If you value your life . . . be quiet!'

Until that moment Hedra had given no thought to her own safety. Her only concern had been for Rachel and her child. Now all the tales she'd ever heard of bandits who roamed the moors by night intent on robbing and killing innocent travellers flooded her mind.

Her heart hammering beneath the fine green wool of her gown and heavy cloak, she'd tried to wriggle free to see her assailant, but his muscular arm had grasped her firmly and his hand pressed tighter over her mouth.

'They're coming,' he'd hissed, dragging her and her horse deeper into the thicket. 'They'll kill us both if you cry out, so don't!'

Terrified, Hedra had held her breath. She had no choice but to obey this man. The first flickers of lights through the trees sent a chill down her spine. She could hear feet shuffling closer, whispered voices.

From her enforced hiding place she had watched, mesmerised, as a string of donkeys, their legs almost buckling under their weight of sacks and boxes, lumbered past. The stooped figures leading them were taking no chances of being recognised, having swathed their faces in ragged scarves. In the light from their lamps she had seen the glint of cold steel, and realised each man had a knife slung around his middle.

Hedra's hood slipped, and she'd felt her captor's breath on her hair. Her face was pressed hard against his chest and, even through the thickness of his leather doublet, she could feel his heart thudding. Was he one of them? — surely he must be — how else would he have known these men were here?

She'd been rigid with fear, but now that the immediate danger had apparently passed, she had to escape this bandit and race to fetch Dr Roskilly. She had tried to struggle free and, to her surprise, he'd released his grip. She stepped back, searching the outline of his face, taking in the high cheekbones, the firm line of his jaw. There was something familiar about the tilt of this man's head. But how was that possible when he was a stranger?

She glanced up and saw a flash of white teeth as he smiled down at her.

'Don't worry. I'm not going to murder you.' His eyes had followed the track the smugglers had taken. 'Although they would have if they'd caught you,' he said, turning back to her.

She couldn't help wondering what colour those dark eyes really were.

'Why were you flying through the night like a hellcat anyway?' he asked.

Panic had returned at the memory of Rachel's pain-contorted face.

'Dr Roskilly!' she had cried, frantically looking round for her mare. 'I must get to Dr Roskilly's house. My brother's wife is very ill.'

She felt the man stiffen. He was matching her urgency. 'Here, I'll help you.' He grabbed Hedra's horse. 'Do you have far to go?'

She nodded ahead. 'A mile beyond the village.'

He had grasped her waist in one easy movement and, as though she weighed no more than a feather, swung her back onto her horse. She seized the reins, but looked back as her mare picked up speed. She could still see the outline of his tall frame in the darkness.

'Good luck to your sister . . . ' he had called after her, but the rest of his words were snatched by a gust of wind as he watched her ride away.

★ ★ ★

Now riding headlong into the darkness, Hedra looked back and saw Dr Roskilly narrowing his eyes, peering into the gloom for his first sight of Penmere Manor.

Then, where the track veered seaward, he spotted it, lights blazing from almost every window. It seemed the entire household was about. Even before they dismounted, the great oak door was thrown open and a servant, her white linen cap askew, rushed to meet them.

'Thank heavens you're back, Miss Hedra,' she said, then turning to her companion, 'Dr Roskilly . . . it's this way!' She puffed ahead, picking up the candlestick she had laid aside and hurried him indoors towards the staircase. 'She's having so much trouble, poor lamb.'

But Hedra rushed ahead of them to fly up the stairs and burst breathlessly into her sister-in-law's bed chamber. 'He's here, Rachel!' she gasped. 'Dr Roskilly's here! All will be well now!'

Rachel lifted a limp hand and attempted a smile, but her face, pale from the effort of her labour, contorted into another grimace of pain.

Hedra squeezed a cloth in the basin of water by the bed and mopped Rachel's forehead. 'I've been trying to keep her cool,' she said helplessly,' as Dr Roskilly entered the room. 'I didn't know what else to do.'

'Well, I'm here now, so there's

nothing to worry about.' He put his black leather bag on a chair and his hand on his patient's swollen abdomen. 'How often are the pains?'

'All the time. They're not stopping, doctor!' Bessie the maid had followed the physician and answered for her mistress, wincing at the sight of her discomfort as another contraction took hold.

'Come on now, my dear,' said the old doctor kindly. 'The first born always tends to be the most difficult. So let's get this infant born, shall we?'

And a few hours later the lusty cries of Conan St Neot filled the oak-panelled room, at precisely 5.22am on December 24, 1778.

2

Dr Roskilly was making himself comfortable by the log fire in the downstairs parlour. His bushy grey eyebrows had lowered and his keen blue eyes were studying Hedra. He tutted. 'The men had no business leaving you two women alone with only the servants when Rachel was so close to her time. What was Matthew thinking, never mind young Nathan? He should have been here for the birth of his son.' He sipped from the glass of Madeira wine Hedra had placed on the table by his chair.

'They could hardly have known the child would arrive tonight. It . . . he . . . ' Hedra corrected herself. Now that her first nephew had come into the world he at least deserved the dignity of no longer being referred to as 'it'. 'He wasn't expected for weeks yet. I'm sure if Father had known his grandson was to arrive this early, he would not have gone to Truro with Nathan and Kit for the reading of Uncle Thomas's will.'

'Ah yes.' Dr Roskilly warmed his hands at the blazing log fire and settled more comfortably into his chair. 'Terrible business.' He shook his head sadly. 'How is your father?'

'He tries not to show his feelings,' replied Hedra, wearily. 'But Uncle Thomas was my father's brother, and they were very close.'

'Yes, I know.' The physician was a year older than her father, Matthew St Neot, but they had grown up together and had attended the same school in Penzance. 'I didn't know Thomas all that well. He was older than us, but I remember their younger brother, Edgar,' he continued, pursing his lips as he stared at the flames licking round the logs in the huge inglenook fireplace.

'A right little scallywag if my memory serves me correctly. He wouldn't have given Thomas an easy time. Can't imagine why Thomas and Morwenna allowed him to stay with them at Mellin Hall.' He tipped back the last of his wine. 'I suppose your father will inherit the estate now?'

Hedra shook her head, her shoulders rising into a shrug. 'I don't think he wants it, but we will all know the details when they get home.'

As children, Hedra and Kit had often visited their Uncle Thomas and Aunt Morwenna at Mellin Hall. She remembered the grand house with many servants scurrying about draughty corridors. But it was the harbour she had loved best, and the little shingle beach where she and Kit — and the boy who had befriended them, Jem Pentreath — had played.

Jem was older than her, a tall, dark, gangly youth more of Kit's age, but he never seemed to mind her tagging along. All three of them had splashed in the sea, built forts from pebbles on the beach, and one day, Jem had taken them to his secret cave around the promontory. It had been dark and mysterious, and they'd found crabs under the stones.

She remembered too, the time he had squinted up into the sun, and pointed to a collection of squat stone buildings high on the hill. 'I live up there,' he said. 'That's Gribble Farm.'

The fishing families of Mellin Cove were simple folk, but the respect they had for her Uncle Thomas and Aunt Morwenna was clear. The same, however, could not be said for her Uncle Edgar. She'd heard hints that he'd even had a hand in the fire that had ravaged part of the Hall a year earlier. Morwenna had been rescued by a servant, but she'd never recovered from the experience and had died a few weeks later.

'Thomas will never get over this,' Hedra's father told her, sadly, when he and her brothers returned to Penmere after the burial.

'That marriage was a love match. Thomas was devoted to Morwenna,' her father said. And his prophecy had been accurate. Hedra felt a tear sting her eye. Thomas lost the will to live, and he'd died at Mellin Hall little more than a week ago.

Like Dr Roskilly, Hedra had also been staring into the flames and was startled when he said he must leave.

'You must have some food before your ride back,' she insisted, rising to call Bessie, from the kitchen.

'No my dear, I'll have one more look at my two charges upstairs, then I'll be on my way.'

'It's stopped snowing, but it's still dark out.' Hedra had gone to the window to pull aside the drapes. The storm had passed and a half-moon cast a silvery path on the ocean.

'It was dark when I came and I managed that journey. No doubt I will manage just as well in the opposite direction,' the doctor said, rising stiffly from his comfortable chair and pulling on the thick coat Bessie had been keeping warm for him.

He rode off as the first streaks of light crept over the moors. He glanced back at the handsome old granite manor house, all of its four chimneys smoking. He would have liked such a house for himself and his wife, Sarah.

★　★　★

Rachel was sitting up in bed gazing at the sleeping child in his cradle when Hedra entered. Only the tiny red face of Conan St Neot was visible above the tightly wound shawl.

'Isn't he adorable?' Rachel said. Her face was glowing as she sank back into the pillows, exhausted. 'Nathan will be so proud of his son, won't he?'

'Well you did all the hard work,' Hedra reminded her as she came to sit on the bed and put a hand out to pat Rachel's shoulder. 'You must rest now — you look exhausted.'

'I feel elated,' her sister-in-law responded.

'Very well, elated and exhausted,'

Hedra conceded. 'But either way, you must still rest.'

But Rachel was imagining her husband's face when he returned to find he had a son so early. 'You will tell me as soon as the men arrive home?'

'Of course.' Hedra smiled, wondering what news they would bring. If her father did not inherit Mellin Estate, as they were all assuming, then it might go to Nathan. She suddenly felt sad at the thought of the family being split. More than any of them, Nathan loved Penmere, and years earlier he had taken on the task of managing its farmland.

She turned to Rachel. 'If Uncle Thomas has left Mellin Estate to Nathan, then all of you will be leaving Penmere.'

Rachel's hand moved over the rumpled sheets, smoothing out the creases. 'That will never happen. Nathan loves Penmere. The farm is his life.' Her gaze strayed to the cradle. 'This is our home . . . the place where our family should grow up. I can't see us leaving.'

'But Nathan is the eldest son, so if Mellin isn't left to Father — or if it is and he refuses to accept it — then the estate is bound to go to Nathan.'

'I hope not.' Rachel sighed, still watching the sleeping child. Then she caught Hedra's hand and said quietly, 'Thank you, Hedra.'

'For what? I was useless. You were in so much pain and there was nothing I could do to help you.'

'You were here when I needed you, and that's what mattered. It was so brave of you to ride out across the moors to fetch Dr Roskilly, although I imagine your father might have something to say about that. The moors are not safe at night. Bessie told me there's talk in the village about a cut-throat band of fair-traders who use the coves in these parts to land their illegal cargoes. They think nothing of killing the local fishermen for what pittance of smuggled goods they can pick up.'

She gave Hedra's hand a squeeze and sank back onto the pillows. 'But you're safe and that's all that matters,' she added sleepily, stifling a yawn.

The sky was brighter when Hedra went downstairs to draw back the heavy crimson drapes from the parlour windows.

Rachel's words had unsettled her and she now knew she could not tell her family about her encounter on the moors. She'd been going to ask her father to find the man who had helped her, give him some kind of reward for his good deed. But she knew how angry her father would be if he learned that she'd gone off alone to summon Dr Roskilly when she could have sent Bessie's husband, Jonas, who was Penmere's only manservant. But she hadn't trusted anyone else to undertake such an important task — and as for rewarding her Good Samaritan, well, she wasn't at all sure the man would appreciate that either.

She decided it would remain her secret.

Despite having been up all night, Hedra felt wide awake. She pulled on her cloak and went outside.

The frosty air was invigorating as she drew deep breaths, enjoying the feel of the icy chill rush into her throat. She struck out across the clifftop, the light covering of last night's snow crunching beneath her boots. From the edge of the cliffs she could see the great expanse of horizon. The smell of the sea was everywhere. Each time she stood on this spot she had the irresistible urge to throw her arms skywards for the sheer beauty of it all. The cove's pebbled beach had vanished beneath the snow, but, in the distance, the outline of the path was still visible ... the path last night's scoundrels had climbed with their over-burdened donkeys.

Further still along the coast she could see the smoking mine chimneys. Even now men would be working in the network of tunnels underground.

Edward had told her that many miners walked for miles across the moors each day to reach Wheal Davy. Then they would climb down a shaft, passing level after level of mine workings before reaching the long undersea tunnels to the face.

Hedra had never been down Sir Edward Tremaine's mine, but she knew some shafts stretched far under the ocean and that while the miners worked they could hear the roaring and crashing of the waves above.

She shivered, pulled her cloak tighter around herself and thought of the new St Neot infant, snug in his cradle at Penmere Manor. Last week her Uncle Thomas had died, and this morning his grand-nephew had come into the world. Warm tears slid down Hedra's cheeks as she turned for home.

Her father and brothers would be back soon. She allowed herself a little stab of pleasure as she pictured the look on Nathan's face when told that his son had been born.

Ice had formed in the ruts under her feet and it cracked as she strode across the fields. She had just remembered it was Christmas Eve — and there was work to be done.

3

The house was warm when she got back, and she found Bessie and Ellen, the kitchen maid, already busy at the vast black cooking range. Mouthwatering smells of fresh baking filled the house. A fat goose and two chickens had been plucked and sat ready for the oven, in which trays of sweet fruit pies were nicely browning.

'Life goes on, Miss Hedra,' Bessie said, wiping a plump hand over her hot, damp brow as she stooped to pull a tray of pies from the oven. 'And Christmas stops for no man.'

Assured that they needed no more help in the kitchen, Hedra wandered through the house, restless for the men's return, and flew to greet them at the first sight of their horses clattering up the icy track. She was bursting with excitement to see Nathan's face when he learned of his new son's arrival, but the news was not hers to give. Struggling not to give away the secret, she contented herself with, 'Rachel wants to see you.'

Nathan's eyes narrowed. 'Nothing wrong, is there?'

Hedra gave an innocent shrug as she followed them to the stables, where Jonas took charge of their horses.

'If something's happened I want to know,' Nathan persisted. 'Tell me Hedra! Tell me right now!'

The grin she had been trying to suppress broke through and she laughed. 'Rachel's got something to tell you. I should go up to her if I were you.'

Nathan did not wait for further explanations. He turned on his heel and tore past them into the manor house, taking the stairs in leaps.

'What are you up to, little minx?' Matthew asked, raising an eyebrow at his daughter.

Hedra clapped her hands and danced

round him, her eyes shining. 'Rachel's had a son!'

Matthew drew a hand across his forehead, tiredness from the long ride forgotten. 'Well, what about that?' He beamed. 'Are they both well?'

'Just as well as they can be,' Hedra answered, making no mention of her desperate night ride across the moors to fetch Dr Roskilly.

'This calls for a celebration,' declared Kit, who had followed them into the parlour and was now crossing to a drinks table behind the oak settle. Selecting the decanter of brandy, he waved it towards his father. 'Will you have one, Father?'

'I think I'd better,' Matthew said, sinking into his usual chair by the fire.

Glasses charged and handed round, they all toasted the new arrival.

'Has Rachel decided on a name?' Kit asked.

Hedra sat on the arm of her father's chair and ruffled his hair. 'It was all decided beforehand,' she explained, 'If it was a girl then she would have been Alice, after Mother, and a boy was to be called Conan.'

She thought she detected the glint of a tear in her father's eye as he raised his glass. 'Well, what are we waiting for?' he said, rallying. 'Let's drink to the newest member of the St Neot family . . . young Master Conan.'

Nathan joined them, his face wreathed in smiles, and Kit went to fill another glass for his brother. 'Well, what's the verdict?' he asked, teasingly, 'Is the little chap handsome, like his Uncle Kit, or really ugly, like his father?'

Nathan sipped his brandy and pretended to consider, then threw his head back and roared with laughter. 'He's a St Neot all right — and just as handsome as they come.'

Hedra scowled at Kit. 'Little Conan is perfectly beautiful,' she said.

'When can we see this perfectly beautiful creature?' Kit was still smiling.

'Rachel's still attending to him, but we can all go up a little later,'

Matthew sipped his brandy, enjoying the sensation of the smooth golden liquid warming his insides. *A new life,* he thought contentedly. *Just what this family needs right now.* Seven days ago his brother, Thomas, had died — of a broken heart some said.

Matthew sighed. He was remembering his darling Alice. She'd died giving birth to their only daughter. His eyes grew tender as he remembered his wife's joy at seeing their baby girl.

'She's beautiful,' Alice had whispered, her voice full of wonder. 'A sparkling little dewdrop. We'll call her Hedra.' They were the last words she ever spoke. Kit's voice brought him back into the room. His son had got out of his chair and stretched, announcing he was going for a walk.

'Anyone care to join me?' he asked.

Nathan had gone back upstairs to his new family, Hedra shook her head and their father raised his glass, indicating he was too comfortable to move from his chair.

But when Kit left, Matthew did get up and, glass in hand, crossed to the window to watch his son stride out across the yard in his distinctive long dark coat. Tall and angular, Kit had the same dark hair as the other St Neot men. Nathan was shorter than his brother, but broad and muscular.

Hedra looked nothing like the St Neots. She was her mother through and through, from the burnished chestnut of her hair, to her wild green eyes, the colour of the Cornish seas.

Matthew smiled as he glanced across at her now. She looked so small and fragile gazing into the fire like that, and he wondered what thoughts had curved her mouth into such a secret smile.

Had it only been a week since he'd stood by that graveside in Penmere churchyard and grieved for his brother? But at that time he hadn't known what was in Thomas's will.

And now there was this little scrap of life upstairs, his new born grandson.

Matthew's flagging morale was slowly being restored — and it felt good.

'Are you hungry, Father?'

He'd been so deep in thought that he hadn't noticed Hedra's light step as she came to the window he stood by and took his arm. 'The kitchen is just full of food,' she said, following his gaze to the figure, head bent against the wind, as he strode out towards the cliffs. 'It looks cold out there. Kit will freeze,' she said.

But Matthew smiled and patted her hand, leading her back to the fireside. The brandy was still doing its work and he felt pleasantly mellow.

The last few days had been emotional. He had not been looking forward to the reading of the will. It seemed to him that these things were always done with undue haste. The circumstances hardly allowed time to grieve for a loved one before dividing up his estate.

'Sit down, Hedra,' he said. 'I have something to tell you.'

★ ★ ★

Kit had crossed the top fields and was now following the line of the cliffs. He could see the waves crashing against the rocks below and watched them foaming into the cove where he and Nathan had played as children. Their father had warned them often enough about the danger of getting cut off by the fast tide, but that had only made the shingle beach all the more enticing.

The sea air was raw and the icy dampness of it seeped into Kit's bones. His father and Nathan would have told Hedra about the will by now. He'd known from her face that she was anxious for news of it, but, like the well brought-up daughter she was, she would have waited for their father to impart the details.

He'd been walking for an hour and had turned back to the house when he spotted Hedra running full pelt towards him. She arrived breathless, her green eyes shining.

'Father's told you then,' he guessed from her broad grin.

'Mellin,' she said breathlessly, hugging her brother. 'You are the new Master of Mellin. How wonderful!'

He laughed, still not quite able to believe what had happened in the notary's office in Truro.

They walked arm in arm, hardly aware of the sharp wind that tugged at the hood of Hedra's cloak and nipped their noses.

'Tell me everything,' she said.

He pursed his lips as though considering, but every detail was already etched in his mind. He could see the notary's small office, its great oak desk, piled high with bundles of documents, tied with different coloured ribbons.

'Edgar was late, and the notary kept pulling out his pocket watch and scowling at it. When Uncle eventually did turn up, he was dressed in the loudest green jacket I have ever seen.' He glanced up at Hedra. 'Father was not amused and demanded to know why Edgar had come out of mourning so soon.'

Hedra knew her uncle had a dubious reputation, but she was shocked at his lack of respect for the brother who had welcomed him into his home.

'Anyway,' Kit continued, 'after a number of small bequests to loyal servants, we were told that Nathan was to have five thousand pounds, because he has a family to support. And you, Hedra,' he smiled down at her. 'You are to have two thousand towards your dowry.'

Hedra's nose wrinkled, and her chin lifted defiantly. 'I can assure you that I will not be needing that in the near future.'

Kit laughed. 'We'll see, little sister,' he said.

'Never mind about that now,' she said impatiently. Go on with the story.'

'Well, ten thousand was left to father.' Kit bit his lip.

'And . . . ?' Hedra urged.

'We were all waiting for the announcement of who was to be the future owner of Mellin Hall. Edgar was smirking — he clearly thought he knew something that we did not. Then Mr Quick, the notary, began to read the rest. I have a copy here,' and Kit fumbled in his coat pocket and produced a sheet of thick, cream paper.

'Uncle Thomas had written,' he said and went on to read from it. '*You, Kit, will be wondering why you have not so far been mentioned in my bequests; well here is the reason. Mellin Hall Estate has been in my wife's family for generations. It has always been dear to them, so I must honour their memory by providing for its future as best I can. Matthew, I know, does not want it, for he loves Penmere too much to ever want to leave. Nathan, being the eldest of his three children, will, I am sure, inherit Penmere one day. That leaves just you, Kit, and Edgar, to be considered.*'

Kit took a deep breath before going on, '*Edgar is my brother. I believed that by bringing him with me to Mellin when my dear wife, Morwenna, and I married, he would thrive in a different environment. I thought he would appreciate the opportunities that were offered to him. But he did not. Edgar threw back in my face everything I have ever tried to do for him. He is a wastrel and ungrateful and I am ashamed that he is my brother.*'

Hedra gasped and stared at Kit. 'Uncle Thomas said that?'

'He did, and Edgar's face was ashen. He jumped up and brought his fist down on the notary's desk, insisting that Thomas's mind must have been disturbed when he wrote that.'

He cleared his throat and read on, '*I now turn to my youngest nephew, Kit. I already know, from the number of times he has visited me, how much he loves Mellin. He is young, it's true, but he has a strong and sensible head on his shoulders. I feel confident that he will look after the Constantine family's beloved Mellin as they would have wanted it to be looked after. I also believe that he will do right by the families of Mellin Cove and care for their welfare as Morwenna and I have tried to do over the years. These people were our friends and I would want that relationship to continue with the new owner of Mellin Hall. Therefore, I leave Mellin Hall, its grounds and estate, including Mellin Cove, and all things upon it, to . . . '*

Kit turned to Hedra, his eyes still wide with disbelief, 'To me, Hedra. Uncle Thomas left Mellin to me, entrusting that the rest of the family will give whatever support and assistance I need.'

Hedra threw her arms around her bother. 'Oh, well done, Kit. Wise old Uncle Thomas chose exactly the right man to look after his estate.'

'I'm afraid Edgar didn't think so. He was on his feet demanding to know his share. But the notary just shrugged and held his palms upwards. Uncle Edgar had been left nothing.' Hedra clapped a hand over her mouth as her brother continued, 'Edgar's face turned from the colour of stone to puce and he stormed out, shouting that we had not heard the end of it.'

'Oh dear,' said Hedra. 'I almost feel sorry for him.'

'Don't waste your sympathies, sister. It was a very ugly scene. Nathan and father were so angry. At first I thought it was because I had inherited Mellin, and not one of them. But I couldn't have been more wrong. Thomas understood us all so well. He knew Father would not want to leave Penmere and that Nathan would eventually inherit the house. They were happy that Mellin was coming to me.'

She reached up to embrace him. 'Of course they were. I think it's wonderful, Kit,' she said, but she saw his eyes were troubled. 'You are pleased, aren't you?'

He nodded. 'Of course I am. But it's

a big place to manage on my own.' He swung her round. 'I have a proposition for you.'

'A proposition?'

'Come with me,' he said. 'Come with me to Mellin.'

He saw the hesitation in her eyes and rushed on, 'Just till I get settled. It needn't be for long. Who knows, you might even fall in love with the place.'

'But what about Edgar? I hardly expect he'll be pleased to see us.'

'I'll deal with Edgar,' Kit said, his face clouding.

'Can I think about it?'

'What's to consider? You love Mellin Hall. Remember that beautiful garden and all those days down at the cove?'

Hedra suppressed a smile at Kit's attempts to persuade her.

He was right, Mellin Hall was beautiful, but memories could be deceptive and she had only been seven years old the last time she was there — fifteen long years ago.

However, the cove was unlikely to

have changed and she could always treat the whole thing as an extended holiday.

But best of all, Edward would hardly follow her there!

She liked Edward, but he'd made it clear that he wanted more than just friendship and Hedra certainly didn't want to marry him. Oh, he was handsome enough, dashing even, and amongst the miners he employed he was known to be a fair man. What woman wouldn't want to be the wife of Sir Edward Tremaine?

There was only one major drawback — she didn't actually love him.

Getting away to Mellin might not be such a bad idea. The decision was made. 'I'm coming with you.' She grinned up at him.

They strolled back to the house arm in arm and Matthew, still watching from the parlour window, smiled. From the looks on their faces he guessed that Kit had invited Hedra to join him at Mellin and it seemed that she had accepted. He tried to imagine Penmere Manor without them, reminding himself that they would be a mere half day's ride away. It wasn't the other side of the world. He was happy for them.

Hedra spotted her father at the window and waved.

She hadn't given him a thought when she accepted Kit's invitation, yet earlier she'd been the one feeling sad that the family could be split if one of them inherited Uncle Thomas' estate. She hadn't wanted Nathan, Rachel, and baby Conan to leave. But she and Kit were planning to do exactly that. A little stab of guilt began to gnaw at her insides.

'I won't go if you want me to stay here,' she told her father after dinner. 'I accepted Kit's offer before thinking it through, really, and you know I don't want to split up the family.'

Matthew put his arms around his daughter. 'You mustn't fret,' he said. 'And as for splitting the family, well it might be just the opposite. Perhaps it will be like extending our family.'

He gave a long sigh as memories came back. 'Having no children of their own had always saddened Thomas and Morwenna and I suppose that was why they regarded their estate workers and all the people at Mellin Cove as their family.' He looked down at Hedra to gauge how she was accepting this unconventional reasoning. 'In fact,' he went on, 'There's no reason why we can't take on that mantle as well — one big family.' He nodded, liking the sound of what he'd just said.'

Hedra's brow creased. 'You really believe we could do that, Father?' Matthew nodded. 'But Kit and I don't really know any of these people and we would be quite far away . . . '

'Thomas talked so much about the families down there that I feel I do know them. And as for distance, well, it's only half a day's ride. So I dare say there will be plenty of coming and going between here and Mellin.'

Hedra sat back and stared at him. 'You really want us to go, Father?'

He nodded. 'Thomas paid us a great compliment when he left the Mellin Estate to Kit, my dear, because he knew that we would all support him.'

★ ★ ★

That night she dreamed of Mellin. The dark stranger from the moors was there, waiting in the shadows to pull her into his arms.

The next morning she dismissed the dream as fantasy, trying to remember her real childhood holidays at the Hall. But it was so long ago, and the little girl who had played happily at Mellin Cove with Kit and his friend had grown up.

But her mental pictures were returning in more clarity now. She could see the rough stone harbour, the twin-masted fishing boats bobbing at the quayside, the tang of freshly caught pilchards filling the air and the singing of the women as they sat by their open cottage doors mending nets.

The memories were sweet, so why did her thoughts keep returning to that night on the moors, with the smell of leather and the strong hands around her waist as she was lifted onto her horse?

One thing was sure, Hedra thought with a sigh. She would never see her handsome stranger again.

4

Hedra and Kit had waited until the Christmas festivities were over before setting off for Mellin. The January morning was bleak but the family had ignored the damp chill to gather in the cobbled yard at the side of the old manor house. Even Bessie and Ellen had stepped out of the kitchen to wave them off. There was a tear in Hedra's eyes when she hugged her father, but Matthew brushed it away with a smile. 'Mellin is not that far away, and you can come home any time you choose,' he reminded her.

Hedra nodded, her lip still trembling, as her father steadied the old mare and helped her into the saddle. She and Kit turned for a final wave as their mounts picked their way out of the yard and onto the track to Penmere village. Behind them their father's voice carried on the wind.

'Don't forget to keep in touch,' he called.

They kept waving until they had reached the spot where the track turned and the house was out of sight.

They were travelling light, Jonas having driven ahead the previous day with a cart packed with their belongings, and they trotted in companionable silence as they approached the village.

They were passing the spot where the stranger had concealed himself. Hedra had to stifle a curious urge to stop and dismount, to stand on the spot where he had stood, brush the gorse that he had touched, and re-live the memory of those few fleeting moments.

She knew how worried her father and brothers would have been if she had told them about the incident. But at the end of the day, thanks to this man, she had been perfectly safe. She glanced down at the cove path from which the smugglers had emerged and her mouth curved into a wistful smile. There was another reason why she had not mentioned the episode to her family. It was her very own secret — and she felt a warm glow every time she thought about it.

★ ★ ★

Mellin Cove was much as Hedra remembered. A string of stone cottages hugged the little harbour, their low doors opening directly onto the quayside. These dwellings belonged to the estate and her uncle had always kept them in good repair. That responsibility now lay with Kit, and Hedra knew he would honour it.

The wind was stiffening and the smell of salt was in the air as they watched a twin-masted lugger enter the harbour. From their vantage point high on the winding path that led to the waterside, they could see a wide expanse of ocean and the sails of two more fishing vessels making for port.

'The Sally P,' Kit said, shielding his

eyes for a better view of the approaching vessel.

'You know that fishing boat?' Hedra
asked.

Kit nodded and raised his arm to
wave to those on board. 'It's the
Pentreaths' boat. That's Jem bringing
her in.'

Images of the tall gangly youth who
had raced her and Kit along the
pebbled shore all those years ago came
back to her. She remembered how all
three of them would collapse in
breathless laughter as they reached the
mouth of Jem's secret cave. The
thought of having a ready-made friend
in Mellin Cove cheered her, and she
watched in fascination as the lugger
edged its way into the tiny harbour.

Kit cupped his hands to his mouth
and shouted, 'Jem!' He waved an arm.
'Hello, Jem,' he yelled.

The tallest of the three men on board
looked up and lifted his arm in
response. Then he stopped, staring at
the two riders on the quay.

'He doesn't recognise me,' said Kit, waving more energetically.

The strange sensation Hedra experienced as the vessel drew closer intensified as Jem threw a rope to a crewman who had clambered ashore. Satisfied that the lugger was secure, he swung himself onto the quay and walked towards them.

Hedra's heart lurched as she watched him approach. The night had been dark and she had been terrified, but she would have recognised this man anywhere — and from the way he was eyeing her, she was in no doubt at all that he also recognised her.

'Jem,' Kit called, dismounting and walking, arm outstretched to greet his friend. 'Good to see you.' They shook hands and Kit turned to introduce Hedra. She made a clumsy attempt to dismount and Jem strode forward to help her. Her cheek brushed against rough leather; it was the same doublet he had worn that night.

'Miss St Neot,' he said, with a

respectful incline of his head.

'Miss St Neot, nothing!' Kit scoffed. 'You know very well that her name's Hedra. We're all friends here.'

Jem raised an eyebrow and there was an edge to his voice. 'Forgive me,' he said, an undisguised taunt in his voice, 'but I thought you were our new lord and master.'

Kit and Hedra exchanged uneasy glances. 'If you mean I've inherited Mellin from my uncle, then yes.' He frowned and stared at Jem. 'But I've no plans to change anything.'

'Does that include allowing Edgar and his cut-throats to go on running amok? He's the one who has been in charge around here lately, Kit, not Mr Thomas.' Jem's dark brows drew together and he turned his attention to the returning fishing boats.

'I think you'd better explain yourself,' Kit said. 'Edgar is also my uncle and I don't take kindly to hearing lies being spread about him.'

Jem released a long slow breath and

shook his head. Hedra stared at him. How could he say such things about her family?

Then he was moving off, with only the merest backward glance. 'If you'll both excuse me,' he called over his shoulder, 'I have a catch to unload.'

Hedra felt the blood course through her veins. This wasn't the man of her dreams — nor the boy she and Kit had played so happily with all those years ago. This man was arrogant, insolent, and he had insulted her family! She opened her mouth to order him back to explain himself, but Kit placed a restraining hand on her arm.

'Let's wait until we know what this is all about,' he said, grimly.

It took all of Hedra's willpower to bite her lip and stay silent. She glared at the broad shoulders of the retreating figure, the rakish dark hair tied carelessly back, and watched as he climbed back aboard his boat.

Jem Pentreath had some explaining to do!

As their horses picked their way up the winding track to Mellin Hall, Kit was shaking his head in disbelief at the encounter.

'I thought Jem Pentreath was our friend,' Hedra said angrily.

'So did I,' Kit replied, his face serious.

The light was fading as they approached the Hall. Hedra could remember the flurry of activity that had always greeted new visitors; friendly maids fussing a welcome, showing them to cosy bedchambers, delicious aromas of roasting meats coming from the kitchens.

Tonight the place was in darkness and no servants appeared to welcome them. Hedra had an uneasy feeling. 'Something's not right here,' she said.

Kit swivelled in his saddle to gaze round at the dark mullioned windows. 'Where is everybody?' he murmured. It had been less than a year since his last visit, but the place had an unkempt appearance.

They rode into the yard. Through the open door to one of the outhouses Hedra could see the wagon Jonas had driven from Penmere the previous day. It had not been unloaded.

They swung round when they heard footsteps approach from the side of the house. It was Jonas. He nodded over to the wagon. 'They won't let me into the house,' he said with an apologetic shrug. 'I'm sorry Mr Kit, sir, but I couldn't unload it.'

Kit swung himself down from his horse and helped Hedra dismount. 'Who won't let you in, Jonas?' he asked.

The man shrugged again. 'Whoever's inside. I don't know. They just won't open the doors.'

'This is ridiculous,' Kit growled, striding towards the arched doorway. He hammered it with his riding crop. 'This is Kit St Neot — open up at once!'

There was a grating noise and Hedra braced herself as the door slowly creaked open and a rough-looking

49

individual appeared. The man's face was scarred and his clothes were filthy. She winced at his sour smell as he shuffled back, making space for them to enter.

'Baby Kit — and his little sister!' Edgar's jarring roar echoed through the old house. 'Here,' the voice snarled. 'Come here.'

Hedra stayed behind Kit as they made their way along a dark corridor leading off the main hall. No candles had been lit and the building was gloomy. 'Here, I say! Through here!'

They emerged into what was formerly their Uncle Thomas' and Aunt Morwenna's elegant parlour. Hedra stifled a gasp; the room was certainly not elegant now. A single candle burned on the mantelshelf and, by the light of its guttering flame, she could make out plates of half-eaten meals strewn about the room, drapes sagging off their hooks and ash from the untended fire littering hearth and rugs. A splintered chair lay discarded in a corner and their

Uncle Edgar's untidy form was splayed across another.

'Whatever's happened here, Uncle Edgar?' Hedra asked, not quite believing the chaos around her. 'Where are the servants? Why aren't they looking after you?'

'I've dismissed them all,' Edgar rasped in reply, his words slurring. Hedra saw Kit's jaw stiffen as he stared at Edgar.

'It wasn't your place to do that,' he growled.

'No. I suppose this is all your domain now, little Kit.' Edgar rose unsteadily from his chair and began to sway towards them.

'I think you should go to bed, Uncle,' Kit said, moving forward to help him. But Edgar struggled free and staggered to the door, his unsavoury companion shuffling behind him.

'I'm going further than bed, young Kit,' he growled. 'I'm leaving! This house is all yours now.'

They stared in astonishment as

Edgar's bulky frame lumbered towards the open door, which he slammed behind him.

Hedra held her head in her hands. 'What have we come to, Kit? This is terrible. All the village is against us.' She spun round staring aghast at the room, her voice rising. 'The place is a horrible mess and we have no servants to help us clean it up.'

'You have me, Miss Hedra,' said a voice from the door, as Jonas joined them. 'Leave this to me.'

'This is not your job, Jonas. You are employed at Penmere to look after the stock and help with the farm. We don't expect you to be a housemaid.' The man was no taller than Hedra, but he and his wife, Bessie, had looked after the St Neot family's needs for a long as she could remember. She touched his arm. 'Thank you, Jonas. Your offer is welcome, but all three of us will work together to put this right.'

From the corner of her eye she saw her brother's eyebrow shoot up and she laughed. 'Yes, Kit — that means you too.'

On big family occasions Hedra was used to helping Bessie in the kitchen so she was no stranger to hard work and, under her instruction, the parlour was soon restored to a reasonable state of comfort. Kit removed the dirty crockery to the kitchen while Jonas fetched in water from a well in the yard and helped Hedra light a fire to boil it.

It was late when they finished and Hedra collapsed into a wooden rocking chair by the kitchen fire.

'I've checked the upstairs rooms and they look undamaged,' declared Kit, striding back into the kitchen. 'I doubt whether Uncle Edgar ever ventured up there.'

Hedra pushed a strand of hair from her face and stared into the fire. 'Do you think he will come back tonight?'

Kit shrugged. 'When he sobers up, perhaps. But if he does, he will have to sleep in the yard because I've locked the doors.'

5

It was still dark when Hedra woke. She got up and opened the heavy shutters. At first she could see nothing, but she knew this room looked out to sea. Somewhere down there was Mellin Cove.

She opened the window and an icy blast stung her eyes, flooding the room with the sounds of the ocean. Somewhere close by a blackbird was attempting his morning song. The notes were weak, but they were there. She had a sudden longing to be outside, to feel the crack of crisp turf under her feet. She dressed quickly and ran downstairs, throwing her warm dark cloak around her shoulders as she crept out of the house. There was the merest strip of dawn light in the sky behind her, but it was enough for her to be able to make out the curve of the cove. A flicker of light from one of the cottages told her she wasn't the only one up at this early hour.

It had been her intention to walk down the rough path to the harbour, but the ground underfoot was icy in parts and in the darkness she feared she might slip. She pulled her cloak closer and listened, straining for the sounds of more early-rising birds. There was a sound, but not birdsong; a rustling ahead. Hedra stopped and listened again. Someone else was out there!

Feeling suddenly frightened, she looked back to the dark shape of Mellin Hall, but no lights glowed at any of the windows. If she tried to go back whoever was out there might hear her. What if it was Edgar? Locking him out last night would have enraged him. From what she had so far seen of her uncle, he was capable of anything.

In the semi-darkness Hedra spotted the outline of a large gorse bush to her left. She edged towards it, hardly daring to breathe. Then she heard the voices, muffled at first, but definitely getting closer. Crouching behind the bush, praying not to be discovered, she listened to the shuffle of feet, then the voices again. Snatches of their conversation reached her. ' . . . Be quick . . . the luggers . . . torches . . . '

Then a voice she recognised, a harsh instruction spat out. 'Stay down, men! Village idiots never sleep. We finish this now, once and for all.'

It was her Uncle Edgar. In one sickening second of insight, Hedra knew what he and his men planned to do. They were going to burn the fishing fleet — destroy five or six vessels in one go.

She thought of Jem, the pride in his eyes as he brought the Sally P in to harbour yesterday. The Mellin Cove people could not survive without their boats. And here she was, crouching behind this bush, unable to warn them.

The group had crept past her now and as they did so, Hedra spotted the grey shape of a farmhouse in the distance. It was her only chance. She bounded across the cliffs, arriving breathless at the property.

A man emerged from one of the outbuildings carrying a heavy bucket. He came towards her. 'Good Lord, Hedra! What are you doing here?'

It was Jem. Hedra collapsed, breathless onto a low stone wall, pointing frantically to the cove. 'Edgar's men!' she gasped. 'They're going to burn the boats . . .'

The bucket was tossed aside and milk flew everywhere as Jem yelled for his brother, Hal, to join him. The pair tore out across the cliffs and down the path towards the harbour.

'Heavens, lass, what's going on?' A woman appeared from the farmhouse, wiping her hands on her apron. Kindly blue eyes stared at Hedra. She didn't wait for an answer, but took Hedra's elbow in a firm grasp and led her indoors. The delicious smell of new-baked bread filled the warm kitchen and two little faces, peering above a long wooden table, surveyed her with curious interest.

'Sit down, my love, you look exhausted.' The woman hacked off a slice of the bread and poured a beaker of rich, creamy milk, which she slid across to Hedra, before sitting down heavily at the other end of the table. 'Now,' she said. 'What brings you to Gribble Farm?'

Hedra was still trying to make sense of why Jem Pentreath should be here at this farm, then she remembered Kit telling her that as well as being a fisherman, Jem helped his parents, Sam and Sally and an older brother, Hal, run their farm. So this was Jem's mother!

She glanced around the homely room and remembered the collection of stone buildings Jem had pointed to that day on the beach. Gribble Farm might be small, and its furnishings simple, but there was more love and comfort here than she and Kit were enjoying at Mellin Hall.

Between mouthfuls of warm bread and creamy milk, Hedra told her story.

Sally's teeth caught at her lip and a worried frown creased her brow. 'And you say Hal's gone with Jem?' She nodded to the older child at the table. 'Ben, go and tell your father. He needs to know about this.' She turned back to Hedra. 'We're grateful to you for coming to warn us. I know you've said Edgar St Neot is your uncle, my love, but he's a cruel man.'

For the first time in her life Hedra felt ashamed of a member of her family.

'I think the people blame us for the way he behaves,' she said quietly, now understanding Jem's behaviour at the harbour. 'But my family would detest this behaviour as much as anyone here.' She walked round the table and took Sally's hands in hers. 'Please believe me. The St Neots are good people. We are on your side.'

Ben returned with the news that his father had followed his brothers down to the harbour. Hedra tried to picture the scene. She wasn't sure how many men Edgar had with him; not many, she estimated. They would have been counting on the element of surprise.

Had Jem got there in time, managed to rouse the village? She had to go down to find out for herself. She thanked Sally, and after agreeing to her request to visit again soon, left the farmhouse.

It was fully light as Hedra hurried across the cliff top and made her way down the slippery path. This was the route Jem and Hal would have taken. She could only guess at their rage as they tore through the gorse to save the boats. The scene looked normal as she approached the harbour. She counted six luggers, still safely bobbing at their moorings. Women stood by their cottage doors, nodding to her as she passed. A group of fishermen, sharing their own accounts of the earlier happenings, doffed their caps at her approach.

'They're showing their gratitude,'

said a voice from behind her. Hedra spun round and looked up into Jem's smiling face. His eyes glowed with an undisguised appreciation that somehow made her blush.

'Thanks to you, Hedra, we saved our boats.' He was examining her face in a way that made her spine tingle.

Hedra tore her eyes away from his smile and looked round the harbour. Everything looked so normal. 'I don't see any blood — what happened?'

'Edgar and his men took off like the cowards they are when they realised we would put up a fight.'

'I don't understand. You mean they didn't try to burn the boats?'

'Oh, they would have tried alright.' He looked down at her again, and the corners of his mouth curved into a teasing grin, 'But thanks to you, Hal and I got here first and were able to rouse everybody.' Then his face grew serious, his dark brown eyes glinting with anger. 'Edgar thought he could just sneak in with his men and torch the luggers, but we were waiting for him.'

'What if he tries it again?' Hedra's brow wrinkled in concern. 'If I know my uncle, he won't give up.'

'We'll post a lookout from now on.'

The sound of an approaching rider made them both look up and they saw Kit, his mare snorting clouds of white vapour as he galloped towards them.

'So this is where you are? Really, Hedra,' he scolded. 'You must tell someone when you leave the house alone.' He looked across at the high cliffs that encircled the harbour. 'It's really not wise for a young lady to go out by herself.'

'Well, as you can see, I'm here with Jem and I'm quite safe.'

Kit inclined his head towards Jem in a stiff, silent greeting.

Jem cleared his throat and glanced away, embarrassed. 'You have every right to be angry, Kit. I owe you and Hedra an apology for my behaviour yesterday. You could never be like your uncle. I should have trusted you.'

'Yes, you should have,' Kit replied curtly.

Hedra gave her brother a pleading look, and his stern expression cracked. 'But remember, Jem Pentreath,' he said, a smile creasing his face, 'that you will be forever in my debt.'

Jem's dark eyes met Hedra's eyes. 'I already knew that,' he said.

'I must be off now,' Kit said. 'I have to find help for the house.'

'Somehow I don't think that will be a problem.' Jem winked at Hedra. 'I'll make sure everyone who worked at Mellin Hall before returns.'

Kit's eyebrow arched and a suspicious smile twitched at his mouth. 'You two are up to something, I can tell.'

'Don't worry.' Hedra laughed. 'I'll explain everything when I get home.'

Kit looked uncertain, as he turned his horse to leave, but Jem assured him, 'Don't worry, Kit. I'll see that Hedra gets safely back to Mellin Hall.'

He waved as he rode back up the hill, and they watched until he disappeared from view. The harbour behind them had come alive and there was activity all around as the lugger crews prepared their vessels for sail.

'Aren't you going out with the fleet today?' Hedra asked.

Jem shook his head and nodded towards the Sally P. 'I've a good crew and they know what they're doing. They'll manage without me for one day. There's more important things to be done.'

Hedra wondered if she would get in the way. 'You mean you have to help on the farm?'

'No.' He smiled. 'But we'll go up there for a start. Then, Miss Hedra,' he gave an exaggerated bow. 'I'll show you your estate.'

'It's not mine.' Hedra giggled. 'Mellin belongs to Kit. It's him you should be escorting.'

Jem shook his head. 'Kit already knows every inch of this place.' He glanced down at her. 'I'm going to show you the important bits.'

They were heading back to Gribble Farm. There hadn't been time earlier to notice much about the place, but now Hedra looked around with interest. They had passed several small fields enclosed by low granite walls and Hedra counted five fat pigs in one and four solemn-eyed cows in another.

A man Hedra took to be Jem's father came towards them, his hand out-stretched. 'Is this the young lady we have to thank?' His face crinkled into a smile.

'Miss Hedra St Neot,' Jem introduced her. 'Hedra, this is my father.' As they shook hands they were joined by another. Jem raised an arm, drawing him into the group. 'And this is my brother, Hal. He and Father run the farm.'

Hal nodded. 'We caught sight of you at the harbour, but we were on our way back here at the time. We knew Jem would bring you back.' He gave Hedra a respectful nod. 'Pleased to meet you, ma'am.'

'Oh, please call me Hedra,' she replied, blushing.

Hal nodded his approval. 'Are you coming into the house? Ma should have the kettle on at this time.'

'Take Hedra inside,' Jem said. 'While I get the horse ready.'

'We're going for a ride?' Hedra looked around for suitable mounts.

'Sort of.' He grinned. 'You'll see.'

Hedra liked Jem's family, but she couldn't help noticing the children's mended clothes, the basic wooden furniture. Farming such land may not be easy, but there was no doubting the love in this house. The Pentreaths reminded her of her own family.

From somewhere outside came the rumble of wheels, then Jem's head appeared round the door. 'Just how long are you going to keep me waiting?' he demanded, his eyes glinting mischief.

'If you're going out on that old bone-shaker you'd better take this,' Sally Pentreath called after them,

66

waving a thick, woollen blanket. 'You don't want Hedra to freeze to death, do you?' She shook her head and tutted indulgently at her son. 'Just because you don't feel the cold, my lad, doesn't mean others are not more delicate.'

Jem took the blanket and helped Hedra up onto the cart. 'It's not a very elegant mode of travel, I'm afraid.'

'I think it's wonderful,' Hedra laughed, tucking Sally's blanket around her knees. 'Where are we going?'

'A special place,' Jem said, 'You'll like it, I promise.'

The road they took was wider than the bridleways, but just as rough and Hedra felt more than a touch queasy as they rumbled on. To distract from the motion of the swaying cart, she asked about the Sally P.

'I found her in Falmouth. She was in a right old state, but going cheap.' He shrugged, his mouth curving into a smile as he remembered. 'I'm more of a fisherman than a farmer, so I had the family's blessing when I fixed her up.'

He grinned. 'Especially when I named her after my mother.'

'Wise decision,' said Hedra, smiling back at him.

'Well it's a start.' Jem nodded. 'I plan to have a whole fleet of fishing boats some day.'

They'd turned off the main track and were now in a lane, bordered on each side by high overgrown hedges. There was a clearing on the left and Jem directed the horse towards it.

'This is it?' Hedra asked, wondering what was of interest here.

'Just ahead,' he said. 'We have to cross a field.'

The ground underfoot was crisp and there were two stone stiles to negotiate. 'There,' Jem said, pointing ahead. 'I told you it was special.'

Hedra stared, her brow creased, trying to understand the purpose of the stone structures. They were ruins, but looked as though they might have been dwellings in some ancient time. 'Did people actually live here once, Jem?' she asked, frowning at the remains of apparently circular structures.

'They might look inhospitable now,' he agreed, 'but when these houses were built many centuries ago this would have been a high status village.'

She gazed out over the ruins, trying to see the place with his eyes. She hadn't noticed him come to stand beside her. 'Here, take my hand,' he said. 'The ground is rough and the stones slippery.'

At the touch of his fingers, her heart gave a lurch and her legs felt peculiarly weak. He was talking, explaining the place to her, but he was so close that she had to force herself to focus on his story . . . then the words stopped, and he was looking down at her. Hedra felt she was drowning in those melting brown eyes.

Her voice came out in a whisper. 'It was you that night on the moors . . . '

His eyes scanned the horizon. 'I didn't think you'd recognised me.'

She looked away. 'I wasn't sure,' she

lied. How could she tell him that no matter how hard she tried, she couldn't erase that exquisite moment when he had held her close on the moor? Even now her heart was pounding so wildly that he must surely hear it. She'd recognised him immediately of course, even before he'd reached up to lift her from her horse.

'I never thanked you. You probably saved my life.' Her voice sounded strange, as if it belonged to someone else. He was very close to her and when he bent his head, Hedra could feel the whisper of his breath as his lips brushed her cheek.

'A debt that you have amply repaid,' he said softly.

The beating of huge wings startled them back to reality. A large brown hawk had settled on one of the stones. 'It's a buzzard,' Jem said, stepping back from what had so nearly been an embrace.

'A buzzard,' Hedra repeated, limply, struggling to regain her composure.

'He's magnificent.'

Jem scanned the ruined dwellings with brows drawn. His voice was hoarse. 'He probably roosts here.'

Even though he had started to walk away from her, Hedra could still feel his closeness. But the sweet, gentle moment of only seconds ago was lost.

'Kit and I used to come here as boys,' he said, stopping to pluck twigs from nearby bushes and unconsciously snapping them between his fingers. There was a sudden edginess about him and she wondered whether she had said something to anger him?

She thought back over the last few minutes. She'd been expecting more, and he'd known that. Had he found her naïve? She hadn't much experience of men — well, not romantic experience. There was Edward, of course; handsome, determined Edward, who wanted to marry her. He was a loyal friend, but she'd never felt this giddy in his company. She had been foolish imagining that brush of Jem's lips on her cheek had been a kiss.

Suddenly she wanted to get away from this place. 'I'm cold,' she said, gathering her cloak around her. 'We should get back.'

He looked up and she imagined she saw a hint of surprise in his eyes. He threw down the twig he was holding. 'You're right,' he said. 'We should go.'

The journey to Mellin was uncomfortable and Hedra noticed that Jem was careful to keep a gap on the seat between them. They spoke little until they neared the cove and began the climb to the Hall.

Suddenly Jem turned and asked her, 'Is Edgar still living at the Hall?'

Hedra looked at him in surprise. She hadn't thought about it. Last night Kit had locked their uncle out — but he might have taken up residence again. 'I don't really know,' she said, as they pulled into the courtyard.

Kit appeared as Jem helped Hedra down from the cart. 'Just the man I wanted to see.' He strode across the cobbles to greet them. 'Remember that good turn you promised this morning? I'd like to take you up on that.'

Jem and Hedra exchanged glances.

'I've had a message from Father. Young Conan is to be baptised on Sunday and he has requested we return to Penmere for the occasion.'

The thought of being back amongst her family brought an instant light to Hedra's eyes. She clasped her hands. 'But that's wonderful,' she said. 'Of course we must go.'

Then she remembered Edgar. She was in no doubt that he was only biding his time for the opportunity to get his own back on them. If he knew Mellin Hall was unattended he would force his way in and cause untold damage. Her face fell. 'What about Edgar?'

Kit turned to Jem. 'That's where you come in, Jem. How would you like to take up residence in Mellin Hall a while . . . keep an eye on the place?'

Jem shrugged and held out his hands, palms up. 'I can't see why not,' he said.

'I'll be happy to play lord of the manor.'

'What if Uncle Edgar turns up?' Hedra asked Kit. 'It's not fair on Jem if he starts any trouble.'

'Believe me, Hedra. I'am not afraid of Edgar,' Jem said.

'Of course not. I wasn't suggesting that. I just meant . . . '

'Well, if you not, I can always ask my brother, Hal, to sleep over as well. Edgar won't attempt to come if he knows both us are here.'

'Excellent idea,' Kit said, slapping Jem's back. 'Mellin couldn't be in safer hands.'

But next morning, as they rode to Penmere, Hedra felt uneasy. She couldn't stop thinking about Edgar's unsavoury little band of ruffians. Jem had said they were cut-throats. What defence would two brothers have against such villains?

6

The January weather had not improved and as they reached Penmere village the first flakes of snow were falling, laying down a fine carpet that caused the horses to struggle and impeded their progress along the track to Penmere Manor.

But the inhospitable weather was in stark contrast to the warmth of their welcome in the family home. Everyone had gathered in the parlour; even baby Conan had been brought downstairs to greet them.

Hedra went into her father's open arms. 'It's so wonderful to be home,' she said, smiling contentedly round the room. This was what she knew; familiar home ground filled with the people she loved.

After dinner, Matthew St Neot took his daughter aside. 'Are you not happy at Mellin, Hedra?'

'I've hardly had time to judge, Father. It is a very pleasant house, but so cold and . . . well . . . stark.' She glanced across the well-lit room at the family gathered on settles around the fire. 'It's not like this.'

Matthew tapped a new fill of tobacco into his pipe, crossing to light a taper from the fire. 'It sounds like it needs a woman's touch. It's a year now since Aunt Morwenna died,' he said. 'I don't think Thomas had much interest in Mellin Hall after that.'

Hedra sighed. 'I know Kit needs me with him to help run the place, but the house is so . . . ' She screwed up her face searching for the right description. 'Oh, I don't know . . . *hostile*, somehow.'

All evening Matthew had been watching his daughter. She looked the same, yet there was something he couldn't put his finger on. 'I imagine Edgar has something to do with that.' He puffed on his pipe until it caught.

'He's my own brother, but he has always been a bitter, dissatisfied man. Never trust him, Hedra. I would put nothing past him. Just keep him out of Mellin Hall. He has no right to be there.'

Hedra nodded. 'We have someone looking after the property in our absence.' Her voice was hesitant. ' . . . A friend.'

His daughter's tone made Matthew glance up and he saw a look in her eye that told him his daughter truly had changed. He'd noticed a glow to her cheeks that was caused by more than just the bracing sea breezes. In the short time she had been away, his little girl had become a woman. He would ask Kit about this 'friend'.

Hedra had been the first to retire, and in her bedchamber she opened the shutters and gazed out across fields. The snow had eased off, but she was sure there would be another fall before morning. She wondered if it was snowing at Mellin. She pictured Jem asleep there. What bed would he have chosen? Suddenly Mellin didn't seem such a bleak place . . .

Her father was right. It needed a woman's touch again. She would ask Kit's permission to purchase some new furnishings, rugs, drapes, wall hangings. The house needed clocks, mirrors, little polished tables and new utensils for the kitchen. In the spring she would fill it with flowers.

Next morning only the determined efforts of Nathan and Kit to force a way through the snow for the carriages had made it possible for the family to reach the village church. Hedra and Kit had planned to leave Penmere the next day, but the snow was now two feet deep and there was no way a horse could be ridden through it.

The household grew restless waiting for the thaw.

Matthew had difficulty getting out to check the sheep so Kit accompanied him. Several of the animals had got themselves wedged in gullies and would have starved or frozen to death had her brother not made the effort to rescue them.

It was a week before the thaw came. Jem and his brother couldn't have stayed on at the Hall for a whole week. The Sally P would have to sail, and the Pentreaths had a farm to attend to.

The journey from Penmere had taken longer than expected. Melting snow had made the ground soggy, and the horses struggled, so it was dark when Kit and Hedra rode into the courtyard at Mellin Hall.

The former servants had been re-employed and the building was well lit, but Hedra sensed something was wrong. A boy came running from the stables to take charge of the horses. 'Has something happened here? Has my Uncle Edgar returned?' But she knew the answer before the boy spoke.

'Aye, 'im and 'is gang.' A corner of the lad's mouth lifted in a sneer. 'But Jem and Hal saw 'em off.'

'Where are they now?' Hedra asked.

'Thems gone down t'harbour. Been trouble down there, I reckon,' he said, scratching his head.

'What kind of trouble?' Kit asked.

The boy shrugged. 'Don't rightly know the facts of it, but your Mr Edgar's in it, you can be sure o'that.'

Hedra stared at Kit in dismay. 'We should go down.'

'Not we — me,' he said. 'You should go to bed, Hedra. It's been a long and hard day's ride.'

'I'm coming with you,' Hedra called, hurrying after Kit's retreating back. The horses had been taken round to the stables but they had not yet been unsaddled. Kit was mounting his horse as Hedra hurried in. She held up a hand to quell his protests. 'I'm coming too, Kit,' she insisted, beckoning the livery lad to help her mount.

* * *

The scene at the harbour was one of confusion. Hedra could see flickering lamps, dark shapes moving around them. What she couldn't see were any boats tied up. The quay was deserted.

'Where are the boats?' she called, dismounting and running toward a group of women.

'They've gone after Edgar. Him and his men have stolen two of the luggers and the others have gone after them,' one of the women said.

'Which two boats?' Hedra's voice was coming in gasps.

'Bright Star and the Sally P,' another replied.

'That's Jem's lugger,' said Kit.

'It's worse'n 'at,' the woman added. 'Daniel Carny's just rowed in. 'E be a crewman on the Bright Star and they sent 'im ashore to prepare us for the worst. There was a terrible fight out there. Some of the men have been bad hurt.' In the flickering light Hedra could see tears in the woman's eyes. ''Appen some of them be dead.'

Hedra stared at her. 'Is that what he said, this Daniel?' She shook the woman, her voice rising in a shriek. 'Who did he say was dead?'

Hedra felt Kit's hand on her shoulder. 'She doesn't know. None of us will know until the boats get back.' He stared out into the blackness.

Fatigue and distress suddenly overwhelmed Hedra and she sank to her knees. Kit caught her and led her to a wooden seat by a mass of fishing nets. 'Rest here,' he said. 'We'll all know soon enough.'

* * *

Lamps had been placed at the end of the harbour wall and fires lit along the quayside as beacons lighting the way for any returning boats. The waiting families stood close to the flickering flames, hugging their bodies for warmth. Hedra did not join them. The only comfort she wanted was to see Jem's boat sail into view.

Then a cry of, 'Over here!'

Someone was holding a storm lamp

aloft while another fished what looked like a piece of flotsam from the water. But it wasn't flotsam; it was a splinter of planking from the bow of a boat. Hedra stared in horror at the letter 'P'. A cry went up from the crowd and Hedra's hand flew to her mouth. This was the Sally P — Jem's boat!

She felt an arm go round her shoulders and Kit's voice in her ear. 'Let's not lose hope, not yet. Maybe Jem's lugger has just been damaged. He might not even be hurt.'

Kit had meant his words to be encouraging, but the evidence was in front of them. He gave her shoulders a squeeze. 'Come on, Hedra. It's been a difficult day. We should get you home now.'

But she pulled away. 'I'm staying,' she said.

It was the longest night of her life, but as a grey dawn seeped across the sky, one of the village lookouts spotted movement beyond the harbour walls and cupped his hands round his mouth.

'They're coming back,' he yelled.

A ripple of excitement swept the crowd. Everybody edged closer to the water, straining for the first glimpse of what the lookout had seen.

Then the boats were on front of them. Slowly the first vessel emerged from the mist — it was the Bright Star — and it had another lugger in tow . . . the Sally P, damaged and listing, but still afloat. Behind them, the rest of the fleet limped into Mellin Cove's tiny harbour. Hedra could see the outline of a man clamber ashore, then stoop to receive the limp body of another. He turned and walked through the crowd. Two women pushed their way to the front, one of them holding a storm lamp aloft.

'It's my William!' one cried. Hedra recognised Catherine Prado's voice. 'Is he dead?' she gasped.

Then the familiar deep tones Hedra had been praying to hear again spoke gently. 'Not dead, but he's badly hurt. His legs are slashed and he's taken a beating. Edgar's men got to him before we could intervene.'

It was Jem — he was safe! Hedra could feel the life flow back into her veins. A cry of joy was on her lips and her hand shook as she reached forward to touch him, but another young woman got there first. Kerra Prado threw her arms around Jem. 'You've saved my father, Jem . . . you saved him!' In the light of the lamp, Kerra's beautiful face glowed, her eyes shone in almost hero worship as she stretched up to kiss Jem full on the mouth.

Shocked, Hedra drew back into the crowd. Kerra was fussing excitedly round the group, touching her father's face, her other hand on Jem's broad back as her mother led them back to their cottage. Hedra watched the door close behind them and sank to her knees on the wet cobbles. She was only vaguely aware of Kit's arms helping her onto his horse, climbing on behind her, a man's voice from the crowd offering to take care of Hedra's horse until the morning — and then blackness.

* * *

The bedchamber was bright when she woke next morning. The shutters had been pulled back and one of those rare, sunny January mornings filtered in. A maid had brought a tray of tea and toasted bread and laid it on the bedside cabinet. Hedra struggled up from the blankets to murmur her thanks, but when the maid turned Hedra found herself staring into the smiling face of Kerra Prado.

'You are employed here?' The words were ridiculous because the fact was obvious, but Hedra was struggling to put the picture together.

Kerra gave a little curtsey. 'Yes Miss,' she said, 'Have been for a long time, before Mr Thomas passed away, that is.'

'I saw you at the harbour. How is your father?' The question made Hedra feel ashamed because the one she really wanted answered was, *Why did you kiss Jem?*

Kerra went to the other side of the bed and straightened the rumpled sheets. 'Father will live, thanks to Jem. Of course we don't know if he'll ever walk again.' A tear rolled down her cheek, which she quickly swiped away.

Hedra sipped the hot tea and it scalded her throat. She forced the words out. 'You seemed to know Mr Pentreath quite well.'

Kerra nodded and Hedra winced at the secret smile that crept over the maid's face. 'Aye, we do,' she said softly.

When the maid had left, Hedra sat up in bed thumping the pillows. How could she have been so stupid? She had no right to be jealous. What had happened between her and Jem to make her believe he had feelings for her? Absolutely nothing!

He'd saved her from the smugglers that night in Penmere village, but she had returned the favour by warning him about Edgar's plan to burn the

87

fishing fleet. So what if he'd taken her to his special place on the moors? It was the kind of thing he would have done when they were children.

Hedra touched her cheek where Jem's lips had brushed it. *A thank you kiss*, she told herself angrily, *that's all it was*.

It was all clear to her now. Jem had risked his life to save Kerra's father and he hadn't pulled away when the girl threw her arms round his neck and kissed him. It was Kerra that Jem wanted — not her.

Kit wasn't about when she went downstairs. She wandered into the yard, half planning to go for a ride. There was still plenty of snow around, but the bridleway she could see running off across the moors looked reasonably passable. She went into the stable, but only Kit's horse was there.

'Where's Molly?' she asked the stable lad, who had appeared at the sound of her footsteps in the yard.

'Is this who you're looking for?' a

voice asked from over her shoulder. She knew before she turned who the rich Cornish burr would belonged to. She spun round, forcing herself to smile, but her eyebrows shot up at the sight of Jem leading her horse across the cobbles.

'I offered to bring her up,' he said, the familiar grin beginning to curve his mouth. 'I didn't realise you had been down at the harbour last night. I hear you were too weary to ride the mare home.'

'We thought you were dead,' Hedra said stiffly.

His smile widened. 'Were you worried about me?'

Hedra felt her temper flare. The man's audacity amazed her. He was involved with another woman, yet here he was flirting with her. She snatched Molly's reins from him. 'We're glad you got back safely. Thank you for returning my horse.' Then she turned on her heel and left him staring after her in the yard.

The confrontation had gone badly. She knew how unreasonable her behaviour had been, yet she had been powerless to stop it. She believed the man had feelings for her and allowed herself to be flattered. If he'd thought her silly and naive before, then he must think her a complete fool now.

In the stable she stroked Molly's silky mane. Whoever had looked after the animal the previous night had done his job well. Maybe she could salvage some shred of respect by seeking him out to thank him. On an impulse she went to the kitchen, wrapped a joint of beef in a clean linen square and put it in a basket, adding a hunk of cheese and some apples brought from Penmere. Then, snug in her winter cloak, she set off on foot for the village, aware that Jem had gone in the opposite direction to the farm.

She felt guilty about the Prado family. Her only thoughts last night had been for herself and her feelings for Jem. She now realised how difficult life would be for this family if William, the main breadwinner, could no longer work his boat.

The door opened at her first knock. 'I've come to enquire about Mr Prado,' she told the strained face of the woman who beckoned her in. Catherine Prado couldn't be more than her mid-forties, but a sleepless night caring for her injured husband had left her exhausted. Dark shadows filled the hollows under her eyes and her hair hung in dishevelled strands about her pallid face.

Hedra threw down the basket and put her arms around the woman who began to weep silently on her shoulder. 'He'll never sail that lugger again,' she sobbed miserably. 'Our William will live, but he'll be an invalid. That's what the physician says.'

Hedra led Catherine to a chair. William Prado was asleep in a bed on the far side of the room. Four children of assorted ages — Hedra guessed between two and eight years old

— were eyeing the apples that had spilled from Hedra's basket and rolled across the floor.

'They're for you.' She nodded to them. 'Help yourselves.'

The children scuttled across the room in pursuit of the apples and sat munching them as their mother looked on with a wan smile. 'That was kind of you,' she said.

'Nonsense,' returned Hedra. 'We have too much food up at Mellin. I'll bring some more in the morning.' But another idea was forming in Hedra's mind. She'd have to verify with her father if it was possible, but it could be the salvation of this family. And if she put her own feelings aside, she could probably help some others she had recently grown very fond of.

★　★　★

It was a week before her father's letter arrived, but it contained the news she'd been hoping for.

'I don't believe it!' Catherine Prado exclaimed, clasping her hands in excitement and disbelief. 'You really want to buy the Bright Star?'

Hedra nodded. 'My father has advised a fair price for the vessel, so I will offer you that amount on the understanding that this arrangement is known only to the two of us.'

Catherine's shoulders rose in a shrug. 'If that's what you want, Miss.'

Hedra moistened her lips before continuing. 'There's more . . . ' Catherine's eyebrow went up, waiting for the catch in the transaction, but Hedra smiled. 'All I want you to do is to offer the Bright Star to Jem Pentreath and tell him he can pay for it in regular monthly amounts from the value of the extra fish he will catch.'

The woman's brows knitted and she stared at Hedra. 'I thought you said it was you that wanted to buy the boat.'

'That's right, Catherine. But I don't want Jem to know. He must believe that you still own the vessel.' She thrust out her hand. 'Do we have a deal?'

Catherine still looked baffled. 'What if Jem doesn't want the Bright Star?'

Hedra's thoughts went back to Jem's words in the ancient village when he'd told her he planned to own a whole fleet of fishing boats one day. 'I'm almost certain he will,' she said. *Especially when he marries Kerra,* she thought unhappily.

'Well, if that's the way you want it, Miss. Can't say as I understand it, but I'm more than happy to shake on your offer.'

Hedra put a finger to her lips. 'But my involvement is strictly secret — even from your family.'

Catherine nodded. 'You can trust me, Miss,' she said.

Hedra was pleased with her business arrangement. She knew Jem could operate both vessels by putting a member of his crew in charge of the Bright Star. And despite the commitment to the Prados, the extra income from two boats wouldn't go amiss in the Pentreath family. But best of all, Jem would be on his way to owning the fleet of fishing boats he dreamed about.

★ ★ ★

Hedra had taken to visiting Sally Pentreath when she knew Jem would be at sea. 'Has something happened between you two?' Sally asked one day, setting a beaker of milk in front of Hedra.

'In what way?' Hedra asked, her expression innocent.

'I'm not sure,' Sally said, her shrewd eyes questioning, 'You and Jem don't seem to have that same easy-going relationship any more.'

Nothing got past Sally, but even she could never imagine just how dearly Hedra longed for those times past. She shrugged. 'He's a busy man now, Sally. He has two boats and more responsibilities.' *Not to mention the time he spends with his sweetheart, Kerra Prado,* she thought.

Sally sat down and the smile that creased her face made Hedra realise what a handsome woman Jem's mother must have been in her youth. 'Well I can't say the extra money that two boats bring doesn't make a difference to this family. Although,' she added, brushing invisible crumbs from the table, 'I tell him he should save his money, put it away for the family of his own that he will have one day. My Jem will make some young woman a good husband. He has a good mind, and a strong body, and just about the kindest heart of any man I've ever met.'

She got up and produced a bolt of smart brown cloth. 'Jem brought this back from Penzance last week for me to make new clothes for the children.' She smiled fondly as she ran her hand over the fabric, adding, 'And there was a big piece of gingham for me.'

Hedra swallowed a lump in her throat. She didn't need anyone to tell her how wonderful Jem Pentreath was; she only hoped Kerra appreciated him.

'I reckon things are looking up for Mellin Cove too,' Sally said, returning to her chair. 'Especially now that your Uncle Edgar seems to have left.'

Suddenly Hedra was alert again. 'What does Edgar have to do with it?'

'I thought you knew,' said Sally, wondering if she had said too much. 'He brought in this evil band of devils and they threatened the local men that unless they turned a blind eye to his smuggling, he would kill them — and not just them,' she went on, her eyes angry, 'but their families as well.'

'What? Even Edgar couldn't be that evil.' Hedra's head was reeling. Her father had warned her not to trust Edgar but she was sure that not even he was aware of just how sadistic his brother had become.

Sally smiled. 'A sweet child like you wouldn't know about such things, but your uncle is a really wicked man.'

Suddenly it all fell into place. She now understood what Jem had been doing that night at Penmere. He had been following Edgar's men to see where they were taking the smuggled goods. Had the Mellin Cove luggers set sail to recover it? Hedra pursed her lips. She was sure that was exactly what had happened that night.

As she left Gribble Farm and set off back across the cliffs towards Mellin, the wind had dropped and the sea, far off to her left, was now grey and calm. The cove and harbour came into view as she reached the fork in the paths. Glancing down, the harbour looked deserted. The fishing fleet was still at sea. She scanned the horizon but could see no sign of any masts and she knew Jem and the others would be waiting for the next winds to fill their sails and bring them home.

A shiver ran down her back. There had been no word of Edgar since his failed attempt to steal the Mellin men's boats. He could have moved out of the area, as many of the locals believed, gone north to the alehouses of Truro, but Hedra now knew how vindictive her uncle could be. He wouldn't give up. If he really had left the area, then he would be back. She was certain of that. Perhaps he was already here, hiding somewhere nearby just waiting for his chance to get even.

The chimneys of Mellin Hall were visible now and the sight of them helped to still Hedra's feeling of unease. She liked to enter the house through the yard, where she could check up on Molly. Today, however, there was a third horse in the stable; a shiny black stallion she had never seen before. Curious, she went in search of Kit.

She found him in the parlour entertaining a stranger, but when the visitor rose and turned to greet her she was dismayed to find it was Edward Tremaine. He cut a handsome figure in his burgundy velvet jacket, black breeches and brown leather riding boots. His brow rose a fraction as he came smiling towards her and she realised her appearance — her mud-splattered cloak and her hair, tugged from its chignon by her walk across the moors — must have shocked him.

'My sister's gone native, as you can see, Edward,' said Kit, standing as she entered the room.

Annoyed by Kit's teasing ridicule in front of this particular visitor, Hedra accepted the proffered hand and inclined her head. 'This is a surprise, Edward,' she said.

He gave a little bow. 'Not an unpleasant one, I trust? Your brother has kindly invited me to stay a night or two.'

'Really,' she said, darting a glare at Kit. 'Well, as you see, Edward, we are very informal here. I'm afraid we might bore you.'

His eyes were appraising. 'You could never do that, Hedra.'

Kerra served the meal that night, and Hedra wondered if she would tell Jem about the handsome stranger currently residing at Mellin.

7

Edward's few days at Mellin had stretched into a week, but the place was working its magic on him and he was noticeably more relaxed as he and Hedra rode over the moors or walked the miles of cliff paths. Not once had he mentioned marriage, and she was beginning to hope that they could have the kind of friendship she wanted.

His presence at Mellin, however, was less popular with the villagers. They nodded respectfully when he and Hedra rode past or wandered down to the harbour, but she sensed a definite atmosphere of suspicion.

'These people don't like me much, do they?' he said one morning as they stood on the quayside watching the luggers get ready to set sail.

'You're gentry, a mine owner . . . you'll never be one of them.'

'And are you one of them, Hedra?' he asked, watching the far horizon.

'I hope they regard me as a friend,' she replied quietly. She was watching Jem secure a water barrel on board the Sally P. He looked up and she waved, but there was no returned gesture.

Even at this distance she could see his eyes were cold, his expression stern. A few weeks ago she would have believed him jealous of Edward, but now she knew he had Kerra, so why would he care which male companions she chose? Perhaps it was the suspicion thing again. Well, Hedra had enough. Edward had done these people no harm, and despite his grand ways and elegant appearance, he was basically a kind, generous man.

'Jem,' she called. 'I want you to meet someone.'

Jem looked up, his expression dark. He was being summonsed like a servant on his own boat. He turned his back, his fists tightening as he fought to control his anger.

'The lady was speaking to you,' Edward shouted, his eyes blazing as he strode the cobbles towards Jem's boat. Hedra could feel eyes turning towards the men as the gap between them closed.

'Are you addressing me?' Jem had spun round, his face taut. Even from this distance Hedra could see the muscles twitch along the sharp line of his jaw. She hurried forward to place herself between the them.

'I just wanted to introduce you to Edward,' she said quickly, trying to keep her tone light. 'He's a friend of Kit's.'

Jem's eyes flickered over Hedra and he could see she was silently pleading with him not to cause trouble. It took all his willpower to extend his hand. Edward's face still had a look of rage, but despite his anger at this fisherman's insolence he admired the effort he was apparently making to avoid a confrontation in front of Hedra. They shook hands without a word or a smile and immediately turned away from each other.

As Hedra fell in with Edward's quick step, she glanced back to see that Jem was watching them leave the harbour. She'd no idea if he had understood her brief nod of thanks.

The incident had shaken her. She didn't understand why two people she cared about should behave in such a way. They were climbing back up to Mellin before she trusted herself to speak. 'What was that all about?'

Edward's stare never left the path ahead. 'The man was being insolent.'

'Edward,' she said softly, 'Jem is a friend. I don't know why you got so angry with him.'

He stopped and turned to stare at her. 'You really don't know?' Hedra shook her head. 'Well I think you should find out,' he said.

The encounter had been distressing and she could tell by the rigid set of Edward's back that he was still unnerved by the experience. Suddenly he stopped walking and turned to face her. His expression softened. 'You know why I've come here, don't you?' He took her hand. 'I want to marry you.'

Hedra could feel her body stiffen. This wasn't what she wanted to hear. Over the past days they had become friends, good companions, comfortable in each other's company — or so she had thought. Perhaps that was enough for a good marriage; Lord knows, some couples didn't even have that. All Hedra knew was that in the last few seconds, her feelings towards Edward had changed. She no longer felt at ease with him. Marriage was out of the question. But she knew that when she told him that she would risk losing his friendship for good.

'Don't give me your answer now, Hedra. I'm leaving today. All I ask is that you consider it.'

She opened her mouth to speak but Edward placed a finger on her lips. 'Please Hedra — don't say anything, not yet. Just think about it.'

He was right. She had to give his proposal some serious thought. An instant dismissal would have been unfair. So she nodded. 'Very well, Edward, I will consider it.'

Hedra was up early to see Edward off. As they walked across the yard to where the groom had brought his stallion, he touched her shoulder and bent to brush a kiss on her cheek. Memories of Jem's kiss, as they stood in the ruins, flooded back. His lips had set her body on fire, and remembering it even now made her fingers shake. Edward's kiss was no more than a polite social grace but she smiled up at him and wished him a good journey home.

'You could do worse, you know,' Kit said, coming to stand beside her. They returned Edward's backward wave as he cantered out of the yard and watched as he joined the bridleway and galloped out across the moors.

'I suppose he's asked you to marry him again?'

Hedra bit her lip. 'I don't love him, Kit.'

He pursed his lips and his brows lowered in a frown, but he said nothing.

*   *   *

The last person Hedra had expected to see that day was Jem, yet here he was striding up the drive towards the house. The familiar pulse of excitement throbbed through her. She got up from her seat at the window and hurried across the room to meet him, then stopped in her tracks. What was she doing? The delight she felt whenever she caught sight of him was quickly replaced by annoyance as she remembered how rude he'd been to Edward.

Jem was obviously calling on Kerra. Then she remembered it was the maid's afternoon off: Surely Jem would have known that? She waited, listening for the voices in the hall. Then the parlour door opened and Seth, their gardener, came in. He touched his forelock, making Hedra smile. 'It's Jem Pentreath, Miss. Says he wants to speak to Sir Edward.'

Hedra's brow creased. What did Jem want with Edward? 'Show him in please, Seth.'

There was no touching of forelocks with Jem. He strode across the room and looked Hedra in the eye. 'It's your friend I've come to see. Is he here?'

'He is not,' Hedra replied, holding her chin high as she wandered around the room, plumping cushions. 'Will I do?' She turned and found him watching her. Her courage almost failed, but this was Kit's house and she'd have no more trouble. 'Edward was only here for a short visit. He went home today,' she said stiffly.

Jem let out a sigh and stared uneasily at his feet. 'You're annoyed with me,' he quietly.

'How perceptive of you.'

Jem held up his hands as though to protect himself. 'You're right. I behaved badly down at the harbour yesterday.

I've come to apologise . . . to both of you.'

'Your apology comes too late because, as I've said, Edward has left.'

'Then maybe you could accept it on his behalf?'

Contrition didn't come easily to Jem, she could tell, and playing the haughty madam had never suited Hedra, and so she relented. 'Oh for heavens' sake, Jem, sit down and tell me what all that was about.'

He shrugged. 'That's just it. I don't know. That man — Edward — just irritated me.' He looked up and their eyes met.

He knew exactly why his anger had flared. Seeing the handsome, elegantly dressed mine owner so constantly in Hedra's company riled him. But the sight of them laughing together on the quay had sent daggers to his heart. Edward was exactly the kind of man Hedra should marry. He was wealthy, successful, and had so obviously charmed her. He couldn't believe they were merely friends. No man could spend time in Hedra's company without wanting to kiss those soft, vulnerable lips.

He realised she was waiting for him to continue. How would she react if she could read his thoughts? The notion embarrassed him and his voice came out more gruffly than he had intended. 'Anyway, that's all I have to say. I'll be off now.'

He was making for the door, and Hedra knew he'd be gone in a second unless she could delay him. 'Your boats,' she said hastily. 'I understand you have two luggers now.'

He turned and grinned, neutral ground again. 'One lugger, and the promise of another, to be more precise.' He went on to explain the arrangements with Catherine Prado, and Hedra felt a flush of guilt warm her neck. How he would resent her if he ever discovered her secret.

'Who would have thought such a wicked deed as Edgar tried to pull that night would have ended in such a way?'

But his eyes were hooded and Hedra knew he was thinking of William Prado, who would never again go to sea thanks to her evil uncle.

He looked out at the long curving driveway. 'It's a small start, but I really believe I can build on it.' His eyes had a faraway look and Hedra wondered if he was still aware of her presence. 'A few more trips as successful as the last and we should be showing a good profit.' He turned to bestow her with one of his heart-stopping smiles.

But Hedra was frowning. Jem was too cavalier for his own good, often sailing the Sally P out into storms that left the other Mellin Cove boats safely tied up in harbour. 'You will be careful, Jem, won't you?' Her voice was appealing. 'The seas around here can be vicious.'

His dark eyes searched every inch of her face. 'Sometimes,' he said, quietly, 'I could almost imagine that you worry about me.'

Hedra coloured. 'I was thinking of

Sally and the rest of the family,' she said, too quickly.

Jem's smile faded. 'No need to worry about them. I always look after the people I care about.'

They were standing very close; she could feel his breath in her hair, his lips brushing it. She turned her face up to him and suddenly his mouth came down on hers. It was so unexpected that she felt herself sway. The fire of his kiss swept through her and she gave herself up to the delicious sensation of being lost in his embrace.

Then she remembered Kerra — innocent, trusting Kerra. She didn't deserve to be treated like this. Hedra attempted to struggle free, but Jem held her tight. 'It's fine, Hedra,' he whispered into her hair, stroking her face. 'No one will disturb us. Kit's out on the moors. I saw him as I came in.'

Hedra slid her hands onto his chest, over the rough leather of his jacket and pushed him away before fleeing the room. She had to be away from him, far away. She couldn't be trusted alone with this man. How could she do this to Kerra — how could he?

She sat in her room, longing for the wind of the moors in her hair, but if she went out Jem might follow her and she desperately needed to be alone.

Her head was so full of emotions she couldn't think straight. She had been proposed to by one man and kissed — her first real, devastating kiss — by another. But Jem wasn't just any other man and she knew for certain now that she could never marry Edward, for no matter how deep a friendship they might share, it would never equal the giddy joy of totally giving herself to the man she truly loved.

Hedra was in no doubt now that she loved Jem, and she put her head in her hands. What a mess, what a ridiculous situation she had got herself into. She could hurt so many others and end up being hated by all the people she cared about. She felt like a prisoner in her own room, but dare not venture out for fear of meeting Jem. How could she ever face him or Kerra again?

It was late afternoon and the light was beginning to fade. She closed the shutters and went back to bed, drawing the blankets around her.

The sound of hooves on the driveway woke her. At first she thought it was morning, then she remembered . . .

Curious about the visitor, she went to the window and pulled open the heavy wooden shutters. It was a clear starry night and an almost full moon danced silvery patterns on the sea. No candles were lit but enough moonlight was shining through the window for Hedra to see her way to the door. She reached the top of the stairs when she heard Kit's raised voice, the urgency in it set alarm bells ringing.

'I'll ride back with you,' he was saying, then she heard him call to Seth to saddle his horse.

Hedra flew down the stairs. 'What's happened? Where are you going?'

'There's trouble down at the harbour. The villagers have got wind that the revenue men are on their way to search the boats. They want me down there to speak for them.'

'I don't understand,' said Hedra, confused. 'Why should the men worry if their boats are searched? Fishing isn't illegal.'

'No, but smuggling is,' Kit said grimly.

Hedra's mouth gaped. 'Smuggling?' Her voice rose in disbelief. 'The Mellin Cove men have been smuggling?' She shook her head. 'Jem would never condone this . . . why didn't he stop them?'

'He's tried to warn them, he told me so often enough, but the fishermen see the French contraband as a way of getting easy money.'

'Dangerous money, more like,' Hedra scowled as she spun round, calling for their groom to saddle up her horse. 'I'm coming with you, Kit.'

'Didn't you hear me?' Kit said,

struggling into his heavy topcoat. 'I said there was trouble. I don't want you down there. It might be dangerous.'

'I'm coming,' Hedra insisted. 'If you don't let me ride with you I'll walk!'

'You're impossible.' Kit shook his head. 'If you're coming we leave now.'

A frost was settling, tingeing the gorse with a sparkling white rime, as they galloped towards the harbour. Hedra had no idea what help she and her brother could be in this as yet unknown situation, but she simply couldn't remain at the Hall.

As they cantered onto the harbour it seemed that bedlam had erupted. Jem's wagon was on the cobbles and men and women had formed a chain and were passing sacks and barrels hand to hand from various luggers to the wagon. She could see Jem directing operations and was horrified — they would all be caught red-handed and she had visions of the entire village being locked up.

Worse still, if the revenue men sent in soldiers now, they would assume that

Jem was their ringleader. Cornishmen had been hanged for less. They must get this cargo off the quay and out of sight.

She rushed forward, yelling above the melée, 'Jem . . . Jem . . . where are you taking this?'

His head jerked up. 'Hedra, get out of here! Go back home!'

'I want to help, Jem. Tell me what to do.'

His eyes searched for Kit. 'Get her home. This is no place for her.'

But Hedra yelled at him again. 'Where are you taking this wagon?'

If they had been reported to the authorities, then someone had been spying on them — someone who would know all the hiding places.

'Not sure yet. We just have to get the stuff away from here.'

She cupped her hands to her mouth and shouted above the surrounding panic. 'Take it to the Hall!'

'No!' he yelled. 'I'm not involving you.'

Then Kit stepped forward. 'It's your only chance, but we have to get out of here now!' Jem heaved the last sack onto the wagon, and in one easy move leapt on board. 'Follow me!' Kit shouted, reining in his horse.

Jem cracked the whip and the heavily loaded wagon rumbled off, gathering speed as it reached the icy track. Hedra held her breath, praying the horse would not lose its footing and pitch the wagon and its contents across the dark hillside.

Only when she was satisfied that they had successfully negotiated the dangerous track did she turn back to the villagers. 'Please go back to your homes,' she urged. 'Everything here must look completely as usual.'

Heads nodded and the crowd began to disperse into the quayside cottages. When she was satisfied that the place was deserted Hedra pulled on her reins, urging Molly back up the hill to Mellin Hall.

Kit had instructed that the illicit

cargo be stored in the wine cellar and every member of staff had turned out to help carry it there. Jem's wagon was stowed in the coach house.

'The soldiers are bound to come here asking questions. I can't leave you to face an interrogation on your own,' Jem said.

'We're in no danger,' Kit replied. 'If they come, it will only be to warn us that dangerous smugglers are about.' He grinned at Jem. 'Get yourself off home. Everything must appear normal.'

'He's right, Jem. You must go.' Hedra touched his arm and for a moment their eyes met. She knew he was about to protest again, so she gave him a little push towards the door. 'It's safest for all of us if you just go back to the farm. They might search there and your family will be upset.'

'You are true friends,' he said. 'Mellin Cove will not forget this.'

8

It was an hour before they heard the sound of horses and the thunder of many feet in the driveway. Kit had instructed Hedra to go to bed so that everything in the household would appear as usual. She held her breath and watched through a gap in the shutters as the red-coated soldiers marched up the drive. The sound of voices rose up from the stairs. The unwelcome visitors were in the hall.

She strained to hear but could only make out snatches of conversation. 'Criminals at large . . . smugglers . . . in danger . . . lock your doors.'

For what seemed like an age, Hedra stood shivering in the darkness of her room. *Please let them go away . . . please don't search the house!*

Eventually, when she could stand the suspense no longer, she stripped off her day clothes and hurriedly changed into her fine cotton nightgown, pulled on her white silk wrap and went downstairs, rubbing imaginary sleep from her eyes and appearing annoyed to have been woken so ungraciously.

Two of the soldiers were in the hall, muskets propped against the wall. They sprang to attention as Hedra descended the stairs and entered the parlour. An officer was seated in the chair opposite Kit. Each had a full brandy glass in his hand, and both rose as Hedra came in.

'Captain Truscott, this is my sister, Hedra.'

The Captain smiled and gave a little bow.

'I'm so sorry, my dear,' Kit continued. 'Did we wake you?'

Hedra rubbed her eyes again. 'There are soldiers in the drive. Has something terrible happened?'

'We came to warn you,' Captain Truscott said, his eyes travelling over Hedra's night attire. 'We've had reports of smuggling in these parts.'

Hedra's hand fluttered to her throat and she gazed at the Captain in what she hoped was wide-eyed alarm. Out of the corner of her eye, she saw Kit's eyebrow arch. 'We're not in any danger, are we, Captain?'

'That's why we're here, Miss St Neot,' the officer said, with an openly appraising smile, 'to ensure that you are not.'

'Well, thank heavens for that,' Hedra said, fluttering her lashes. 'I feel quite relieved. It's comforting to know that you — and your men, of course — are looking after us.'

The Captain drained his glass, stood, and gave a little click of his heels. 'My apologies for disturbing you, Miss.' He turned to Kit. 'Sir.'

'Please don't apologise. We're very grateful, aren't we, Kit?' Hedra said.

Kit got to his feet and nodded. 'Yes, indeed, we thank you, Captain. We appreciate your warning and will certainly keep all our doors locked.'

They both watched as the soldiers

left before collapsing into chairs, convulsed with relieved laughter.

'I didn't know you were such a good actress, little sister,' Kit said, raising his glass to her.

Hedra giggled. 'Me neither.'

With the drama of the night's events still ringing through her head, Hedra slept better than she had expected and woke next morning in good spirits. She stretched before jumping out of bed to cross the room and open the shutters. The cloudless night had given way to a bright dawn, and the sky behind Mellin Hall was already streaked with pink.

An animated Kerra appeared with her tea tray. 'The whole village is talking about the way you and the master helped them last night.'

'Not too loudly, I hope,' Hedra said with a mischievous grin. 'We don't want the soldiers back again.'

Kerra laid down her tray and went on breathlessly. 'They searched all the boats, you know, even came into the cottages, emptying cupboards, pulling

up floorboards, frightening everyone to death.' Her eyes were wide and she smiled. 'But they found nothing.' Her words trailed off and, for a second, Hedra thought the girl was going to dissolve into tears.

'It really is fine now, Kerra. The soldiers won't find anything, not now that they've stopped searching.'

'It's not that,' Kerra said, and her body shuddered as a tear really did roll down her cheek. 'They ripped up all my things.' Her words came in little bursts. 'My dowry things . . . in my trunk . . . one of the soldiers . . . he put his bayonet through them . . . '

Hedra's eyes widened and she stared at the maid. 'Your dowry? You're getting married, Kerra?' The guilt Hedra felt about her feelings for Jem, and that one moment of weakness when she had abandoned herself to his kiss, was nothing compared to the despair that now swept through her. Kerra and Jem were getting married. She felt sick.

Why had she surrendered to that

kiss? It was her fault; Jem would never have kissed her if she hadn't longed for it, urged him on with her eyes. Well — from now on it would be strictly friendship between them.

By the time Hedra dressed and went downstairs, Kit was sitting at one end of the long refectory table, a platter of eggs and ham in front of him. 'Sleep well?' he asked, looking up as she walked in.

She ran a hand through her long copper hair. At Penmere she would have styled it high, securing it in elegant twisting strands as befitted a young lady of her class, but today it swung free. From the window she could see the white crested waves rolling in. She imagined them crashing on the rocks around the cove . . . into Jem's secret cave.

'I need some air,' she said, turning for the door.

'I wouldn't go down to the harbour this morning, Hedra. The soldiers could still be around. If they were able to make any connection between us and the villagers down there then they might come back to search the Hall.' He tore a chunk of bread from the newly-baked loaf on the table and dunked it into his egg. 'It will be much safer for everyone if you stay away from the cove today.'

Hedra sighed. 'You're right. I'll take the cliff path and if I see any soldiers, I promise to look the other way.'

Kit's face twisted into a frown and he called after her. 'Just be careful, that's all I ask.'

The path was rocky and hugged the edge of the cliffs. She moved with caution, knowing a careless step could send an unwary traveller crashing to the rocks below. The wind came in gusts, and for a while Hedra stopped to watch the wild tossing of the ocean.

The curve of Mellin Cove was now far behind her and the moors were wilder here; outcrops of boulders covered the terrain, stunted trees bent at an angle to the wind and the gorse grew more thickly. This part of Cornwall was littered with strange monuments and ancient standing stones. Hedra had heard tales of bizarre rituals amongst the stones. She shivered and turned to retrace her steps when a movement in the gorse caught her attention. She froze. Someone was out there, watching her!

Her heart was thudding as she fled, stumbling on the uneven path, more afraid of what was behind her than her fate if she should miss her footing and crash to the rocks below. The cliff path took a sharp bend around a jagged towering rock and Hedra felt her foot slip as she rushed blindly on. The loose stones threw her off balance, but as she began to fall, she felt her arms being grasped in a tight lock, her body being dragged back from the edge. Terrified, she looked up into the face of her captor.

'Are you trying to kill yourself?' the angry voice raged.

Streaked with tears, her face was being cradled against a familiar broad chest, and the smell of leather was in her nostrils.

'Jem,' she said weakly. 'Thank heavens it's you.'

He took her face in his hands and his thumbs gently brushed away her tears. 'You're safe now,' he soothed. His arms around her represented everything that was safe, and she wanted the moment to last forever.

'What happened back there, Hedra?' he asked gently, stroking her hair. 'What were you running from?'

She felt foolish now. The movement in the gorse was probably a rabbit. She had let her imagination take hold and almost got herself killed. If it hadn't been for Jem, her smashed and broken body could be lying now at the foot of the cliffs.

She pulled away and brushed down her skirts. 'Lucky you were here,' she said.

'Not luck. Kit told me where you had gone and I was looking for you.'

'You went to Mellin?'

He nodded. 'You and Kit risked a lot to hide that cargo last night. I thought I'd better move it as soon as possible. That's why I was there.'

That and to see Kerra, she thought, but said, 'Where will you take it?'

'The fewer people who know about that the better.'

The clouds that had earlier threatened a storm, seemed to have rolled away. In their place was a flat grey sky.

'You're not planning to move that lot on your own, are you?' she asked.

'I'm sure someone at Mellin Hall will help me load the wagon.'

'And who will help you unload it?'

'Don't worry,' he grinned down at her. 'I'm strong. I'll manage.'

But she shook her head. 'I'm coming with you.'

'I don't think so.'

The path widened as it swung away from the cliff edge and they could now walk side by side, but they spoke little until they reached Mellin Hall. Hedra stayed out of the way until the wagon had been loaded, but she watched as Jem waved his thanks to Seth and Kit. Before the wagon began to roll she took her chance and leapt up onto the seat beside Jem.

'Come down at once, Hedra!' Kit shouted, striding across the yard towards them. 'Put her off the wagon, Jem!'

'Your brother's right,' said Jem. 'Anyway, it's cold up on the moors.'

'It's fortunate I have a warm cloak,' she said, jutting her chin defiantly.

'Sorry, Kit,' Jem called back. 'Your sister has a mind of her own.'

The cart rumbled out of the yard, leaving Kit staring helplessly after them. They travelled in silence for the first mile, Jem's face a mask of concentration as he urged the horse on over the difficult rough terrain. It was only when they turned off the road into a lane where bramble hedges grew in profusion that Hedra realised where they were going. Jem eased the reins and his horse lumbered into the clearing by the old ruins — Jem's special place. Where else would he have taken his friends' illicit cargo?

Without warning he said, 'Hold on — I'm taking the cart across the field.'

The heavy wagon pitched and Hedra screamed. 'We'll tip over, Jem.'

But he laughed. 'Have faith, woman,' he yelled back over the noise of the wheels. 'I've been driving this thing since I was twelve.' The wind had caught his hair and tugged it free from its tie. His face was animated, his teeth gleaming white. He was enjoying himself.

Hedra didn't risk breathing again until they had come to a halt by the ruins, where Jem planned to hide the contraband. 'You could have killed us,' she accused, her eyes blazing.

But he shook his head, smiling. 'You were perfectly safe,' he said, lifting her down. She shot him a fiery glance.

He had not removed his hands from her waist and looked down at her as he said, 'You will always be safe with me, Hedra. I thought you knew that.'

The tenderness in his voice melted her heart and she knew if she looked at him again she would be lost.

She pulled away, shaken; her heart pounding. He mustn't see the colour rising in her cheeks. 'Let's get started,' she said, firmly. 'Where are we putting this stuff?'

He pointed to the ruins and an entrance to what looked like an underground cavity. 'That's the best place,' he said.

Hedra pushed her heavy clock back over her shoulders. 'The barrels will be too heavy for me, but I can carry some of these sacks.'

'Would it make any difference if I told you to sit over there?' She gave him a long meaningful look through curved lashes. He grimaced back at her. 'No, I thought not,' he said.

The light was beginning to fade by the time they had stacked everything in its hiding place.

'I should get you home,' Jem said.

The physical effort of lifting and

carrying such heavy loads now began to tell and Hedra's shoulders sagged. She was aware of Jem watching her, and if he tried to kiss her now there was no way she could have resisted him. But when he gathered her into his arms it was to lift her onto the hard wooden seat of the cart. 'Not the most comfortable of rides,' he said, moving round the wagon to climb up to his place beside her. 'But I'll try to make it as painless as possible.'

The urgency of their task had given Hedra no time to reflect on her feelings. Her earlier fatigue was mellowing and the movement of the wagon was making her pleasantly drowsy. When Jem spoke, his voice startled her.

'You never did tell me what you were running from this morning.'

She shrugged. 'Nothing . . . a rabbit, probably, I don't know. I thought I saw something move in the gorse.' She glanced up at his strong profile. 'You know how eerie it can be out there. My imagination just took over.' But now that the experience was behind her, Hedra could picture the scene more clearly and it hadn't been just a movement, or a rabbit. There had been someone crouching in the gorse, someone hiding, someone watching her.

Jem had fallen silent and Hedra turned to find him studying her. 'You're quite a brave young woman, aren't you, Hedra?' At that moment she felt anything but brave. 'What you and Kit did for us last night was nothing less than heroic,' he said.

She giggled to cover her embarrassment. 'Slight exaggeration, but thank you anyway. We could hardly let the revenue men seize Mellin Cove.' She cleared her throat before asking more somberly, 'Why do they do it, Jem — get involved in smuggling? Surely they can make a fair living from the fishing without breaking the law?'

His eyes were already narrowed against the wind and she could see his jaw tense. 'Smuggling is a curse,' he said. 'The men believe they're doing it to help their families, but there's not one wife in Mellin Cove who would agree with that.'

'But it's so dangerous,' she gasped. 'Even I know there's a difference between the revenue men's fast cutters and a lugger. If they were caught they would certainly lose their boats and probably be thrown into Bodmin Jail.' She stopped, her hand at her throat. 'They might even hang them.'

'I've tried to tell them,' he shrugged, 'but if they won't listen to their own wives what chance do I have?'

'I'd no idea they could be so greedy,' Hedra said.

Jem turned on her, his voice sharp. 'It's Edgar St Neot who's the greedy one. He was so anxious to grab all the fair trading business for himself that he used to sabotage the boats, mine included, He'd cut our nets, rip our sails, and generally make it difficult for us to work.'

Hedra shivered. The thought of a

member of her family being capable of such deeds horrified her.

As though he'd read her mind, Jem went on, 'It's not your family's fault that you have such an evil and spiteful relation. Any contraband he takes is for his own gain. At least the Mellin Cove men shared everything and made sure each family got an equal cut.' He glanced down at her. 'And before you ask, the answer is no. I never accepted any of it. I earn an honest living from my fishing, and that's the way it will stay.'

'I didn't imagine anything different,' she said, nurturing a secret smile.

'Anyway,' he went on, beaming down at her. 'I have my own plans and buying the Bright Star is just the beginning. One day I will own a whole fleet of fishing boats.'

He was planning a future for himself and Kerra. Hedra could feel the black cloud descending. She'd promised herself she'd never raise the subject with him, but now she felt that she must. 'What about your wife, when you have one that is, Jem? Wouldn't she have something to say about all of this?'

He gave her a curious look. 'I have no wife,' he said.

But Hedra persisted. 'Not at the moment, but perhaps one day . . . '

Even in the darkness she could see the muscles in his jaw tense. 'Everything I do is for the woman I love,' he said quietly.

Hedra's heart sank and she turned away to blink back the sting in her eyes. He was being cruel, and he probably didn't even realise it. How could she bear to see Jem marry Kerra?

The lights of Mellin Hall were ahead of them now and Hedra sat rigid as the cart rumbled into the courtyard. Before he could come round to help her, Hedra scrambled down.

'It's getting cold now,' she said. 'So I'll wish you goodnight.'

She hurried into the house, aware that he was staring after her. The last thing she wanted was to see Kerra running out to greet him.

9

Kit's face was white with anger, and he struggled to keep his voice even. 'So you're back! That was an unbelievably foolish thing to do, Hedra. What if the soldiers had stopped you with Jem's cart loaded up with all that illegal cargo?' He was pacing the floor trying to keep hold of his temper. 'Do you know what would have happened to you? And just how do you suppose I could have explained that to Father — or have you forgotten he has entrusted me to look after you?'

Hedra shrank back as though her brother had struck her. Kit had never spoken like this before and the force of his anger shocked her. Was he right? Had she thrown care to the wind when she went chasing after Jem? Everything he did had an element of danger and she'd wanted to share in that adventure, to sit close to him on the wagon, be alone with him.

The consequences of being intercepted by the soldiers never entered her head. Not that she would have minded for herself . . . not if she'd been with Jem. But an image of her father, contentedly smoking his pipe by the fire, came into her mind and a hot tear rolled down her cheek. Kit was right; it had been completely irresponsible of her not to have considered them. Her bottom lip trembled and she caught at it with her teeth, in a vain attempt to keep her composure, but the tears were already flowing. 'I'm sorry, Kit,' she stammered. 'I'm so sorry . . . ' She'd never felt so miserable.

'I'm not yet ready to end the subject.' Kit came forward, his voice still frosty. 'The worse part of this is that you now know the whereabouts of Jem's stash, where he always takes it, for all I know. It was just as irresponsible of him to have taken you with him.'

Tears were coursing down Hedra's

face now and her shoulders stooped with fatigue. 'Please don't blame Jem. The fault was mine. It was my decision to go with him.'

Kit's expression softened. 'You're exhausted,' he said, coming forward to put his arms around his sister. 'You must realise that while you're here at Mellin, I am responsible for you.'

She pulled away. 'You and Father think I'm still a child.' She looked up at him, her tears mingling with the dust of the day's travels. 'I'm twenty-two!' Instinctively, her foot stamped the floor.

Kit was smiling now. 'Well, right now, little sister, you look about ten.' He turned her round and gave her a little push towards the staircase. 'I'll send a maid up with some supper on a tray — and a jug of hot water. I think you should wash that grime off before you retire.'

A little of Hedra's misery had eased by the time she reached her bedchamber. The maid who brought the water, and returned minutes later with milk and a plate of chicken, bread and cheese on a tray, was not Kerra. It was the girl who helped their cook in the kitchen.

'Thank you, Sarah,' she said, indicating a place by the side of the bed for the tray. 'Is Kerra not working tonight?'

Sarah nodded. 'She was, earlier, but she's gone home now. She'll be back in the morning.'

This was a very small concession from the gods. Kerra's sympathy was something Hedra did not need tonight — or deserve, she thought unhappily.

★   ★   ★

Next morning the sun was shining. Hedra got out of bed and went to throw open the window, letting in a rush of invigorating salty air. It cleared her head but didn't shift her lingering melancholy.

She dressed quickly and joined Kit in the dining room. Only when the warm plate of eggs that had been scrambled with thick slices of deliciously smelling bacon was place in front of her did Hedra realise how hungry she was. They ate in companionable silence and Hedra waited for the plates to be cleared before broaching the subject of last night's angry scene.

'I'm truly sorry, Kit,' she said in a voice so quiet it was almost inaudible. 'And you are right. I did behave badly. I should not have gone with Jem.' She met her brother's eyes. 'But it was my decision to go, not Jem's. So please attach no blame to him for this.'

Kit's chair creaked as he leaned back, his fingertips pressed together as he considered his words. 'Harsh things were said last night and you're right; you should certainly not have gone, Hedra.' He shrugged. 'But I know what a headstrong sister I have, so I don't blame Jem. Anyway, it's past now and best forgotten.'

Hedra left her seat and ran smiling to lock her arms around Kit's neck. 'Did I mention that I have the best older brother in the world?'

'You have,' he grinned, disentangling himself. 'But I suspect you've said the same to Nathan over the years. Anyway, sister dear,' he got up chuckling as he made for the door, 'I have work to do, and calls to make so I'll be all over the estate today.' He paused and turned to give Hedra a severe look. 'Can I trust you not to get into trouble on your own?'

She smiled back and gave him an assuring nod. But after Kit left, Hedra found herself wandering restlessly around the Hall. She knew Kerra would be working somewhere around the property and remembered again the girl's distress at the soldiers destroying her dowry box. Then the thought struck her. She could replace some of the things Kerra had lost.

She went to her room, wondering what went into such boxes. Sally would know, but Hedra dismissed that idea immediately. Sally would soon be Kerra's mother-in-law; she could not be consulted about this.

Perhaps she could just give Kerra something pretty to wear. Hedra went through the row of hanging gowns. She hadn't brought all of her things to Mellin. Most of her gowns were still in her dressing room at Penmere Manor. Besides, she thought, tossing the fine brocades aside, she couldn't give Kerra something she had worn. What if she was insulted?

Then she remembered the shawl Bessie had given her when she and Kit had returned home for baby Conan's baptism. It was still in the trunk. Bessie said it was the colour of the heather moors in autumn, and Hedra had no problem spotting it amongst the folds of her silk night attire. She pulled out the shawl and held its softness to her cheek. It was perfect. She thought even Bessie would approve of this gesture.

Her step was light as she walked down to the harbour, stopping at the point where she had a clear view of the quay. There were no vessels tied up and when she lifted a hand to shade her eyes and scan the ocean she could make out the billowing sails and unmistakable shape of five luggers.

Satisfied there would be no chance of an unexpected meeting with Jem she hurried on, pleased that the weather was so fine for the Mellin Cove fleet. At this time of year, the fishermen had to take every chance they were given. She looked out again at the boats. In a strange way she couldn't explain, it comforted her to see them out there. Despite everything that had happened, she felt part of this community.

Catherine Prado opened the door at her first knock and immediately Hedra sensed something was wrong. 'Is it William?' she gasped, taking Catherine's arm and leading her inside. But William was sitting in his chair by the fire. He tapped his forelock to her.

'Mornin' Miss Hedra,' he said. 'Take no notice of wife. She's just fretting about weddin'. It's the end of next week.' He looked across to Catherine

and scowled. ''Appen she be gettin'
jumpy.'

The familiar dagger embedded itself
in Hedra's heart again. 'That soon?'
She swallowed hard. 'I didn't realise . . .
Jem's a good man.'

They both stared at her. 'Jem? What's
he got do with it?'

'Quite a lot I should think, if they're
to be married next week.'

William's laugh could have raised the
roof.

'Don't know where you got that idea
from,' Catherine said. 'It's Sal —
Daniel Carny's boy, Sal — that our
Kerra be marryin'.'

Hedra dropped her parcel. Kerra
wasn't marrying Jem! She opened her
mouth to speak but no words came.
She realised she was smiling, her eyes
shining. She had to control this
excitement or she would look a
complete fool in front of Kerra's
parents.

Trying to regain her composure, she
murmured, 'I'm so happy for them.'

146

She bent to retrieve her parcel. 'This is for Kerra.' Was she still grinning? 'It's not a wedding present, it's just something for Kerra. She was so upset at what the soldiers destroyed, well, I thought this might cheer her up.'

'That's right kind of you, Miss,' Catherine said, casting an uneasy glance across the room at her husband.

'You better tell 'er, wife. She be bound to find out.'

Hedra looked from one to the other. 'Tell me what?'

Catherine bit her lip, her worried stare fixed on the tiny window with it's view across the harbour to the masts of the bobbing fishing boats. 'It's about our little arrangement . . . about the Bright Star, I mean . . . Jem knows.'

'Knows? What does he know, Catherine?'

'Knows it was you that put up the money.'

Hedra's elation of moments ago vanished as she stared at Catherine.

'You told him?' She shook her head, attempting to clear it, trying to work out what this would mean. 'What did he say?'

Another look at William. 'He wasn't pleased.'

'Tell 'er truth, woman,' William, his voice more sympathetic now. 'The boy was ragin'. Catherine didn't know how to tell 'ee.'

Hedra's hand went to her mouth. The little spark of hope that had soared just seconds earlier had vanished, crushed beneath the certainty that Jem now believed she had lied to him, or if not actually lied, then wilfully misled. She shook her head. He would never forgive her for this.

'He came with 'is money, you see,' Catherine stammered, hardly daring to look at Hedra. 'Gave double what he usually pays, said he wanted to get the lugger paid off as soon as possible.' She glanced up, but Hedra was staring at the floor, her head shaking in disbelief. 'Said he had some special reason to own the boat outright as soon as he could.'

Hedra thought of the smuggling haul she had helped Jem hide in the ruins. Had he meant to use his share to pay for the Bright Star? She was hardly listening to Catherine, but the woman was finishing her story, her voice full of remorse. 'So help me, Miss Hedra, it just came out.' Catherine paused, remembering. 'I said it wasn't ours to sell.' She shrugged miserably. 'He wouldn't leave it alone so I had to tell him the whole story.'

Hedra stared back at the two stricken faces and forced a smile. 'Please don't blame yourselves. It was bound to get out someday.' But she so wished that she had had the chance to tell Jem herself.

Only minutes ago she had held the world in her hand. Jem wasn't marrying Kerra! But now he'd been told how she had deceived him. All hope of him even speaking to her again had vanished. She got up to leave, touching Catherine's hand as she passed.

'Don't worry, I'll talk to him. We'll sort this out.' But just at that moment Hedra had no idea how.

★ ★ ★

The luggers stayed out for most of the day and darkness was falling as Hedra returned to the harbour to meet the returning fleet. She saw Jem at once and waved to him. She knew he'd spotted her standing on the quay, but he turned the other way. She held back as the crews secured their boats and landed their catches. It had been a good day's fishing and he should have been pleased, but his face was like stone.

She waited until the work was done and for Jem to come ashore before she approached him, but he strode past, giving Hedra an icy glare. 'Come to check up on your property, have you?' he growled at her.

'That's not fair, Jem.' She ran after him, trying to match his steps, but he was paces ahead of her. 'Please slow down, let me explain.'

He stopped and turned to face her and his expression said it all. Many interested looks had followed them out of the harbour, but they were out of earshot of the villagers now.

'Explain, then. Tell me why you set out to humiliate me. Was it a game? Did I amuse the grand lady?'

'You're being ridiculous,' she pleaded. 'You know there was no game. I was trying to help, that's all.'

'You think I want to be beholding to you?' His voice was incredulous.

'You! It's not all about you!' she cried defiantly. 'It was the Prados I was helping. How does that humiliate you?'

'You let me believe I was buying the Bright Star from them when all the time the boat was yours.'

'It was a business arrangement. The Prados needed money but they would never accept charity so I offered to buy their boat. You needed a boat and I knew you would never agree to buy it from me if you couldn't pay for it outright.' She stared at him, trying to make him understand. 'I was trying to help everybody,' she said, with a helpless shrug.

Jem's face was white with anger. 'You deliberately deceived me.'

'Can't you see I did it for the best reasons?'

But Jem simply shook his head and turned for home. She watched him climb the hill to the farm, head down, shoulders drooping. He was a proud man — and she had humiliated him.

10

Hedra stood at the top of the hill next morning watching the fleet leave harbour. She knew instinctively that Jem would choose to sail the Sally P, leaving the Bright Star to be skippered by another of his crew. It would be another way of punishing her.

She carried on across the moors, the wind howling as it whipped amongst the gorse. To her right was the Gribble Farm. It was oddly comforting to see the collection of familiar stone buildings, look out over the fields where the animals huddled for shelter close to the low cliff-side walls.

It was a good place, a happy place for the generations of Pentreaths who would have been born here. On that first trip to the ruins, Jem had told her of the family rows when he broke away from the Pentreaths' farming traditions to take up fishing. He'd worked hard, taken chances, and eventually made enough from the smuggling trade to buy an old lugger that he named the Sally P — in honour of his mother.

An involuntary smile curved Hedra's lips. There was no one like Jem; he was his own man. The words lingered . . . *his own man.* That's what she had interfered with. She put her hands to her ears to shut out the howling wind. Now she understood. She could see how things must have appeared to him. He thought she was manipulating him. 'What have I done?' she moaned.

The sails of the luggers were far out now. It would be many hours before they returned and Jem had all that time to fret, to hate herself even more. Looking across to the farm, she realised that Sally would know what to do.

'Thought we might see you today.' Sally grinned as Hedra put her head round the back door into the kitchen. 'Come in and sit yourself down.' She flapped a hand at the two youngest

Pentreaths who sat with open books at the table. 'And you young 'uns can play out in the yard while we talk.'

'Aw, do we 'ave to, Ma?' Jem's youngest brother, Joseph complained.

'We want to stay and play with Hedra,' six-year-old Mary coaxed.

No one at Gribble Farm addressed her as Miss Hedra and she felt as much at home here as in the parlour at Penmere Manor.

'Scoot,' Sally insisted, laughing as her children disappeared out the door. Sally sat down in a chair across the table. 'Why don't you tell me about it,' she said, gently.

By the time Hedra had told her story, the tears were pricking her eyes and she swiped at them. 'What can I do? Will you talk to him, explain that I meant no harm?'

'That's for you to do, lass.' Sally said quietly.

'But he won't speak to me. He says I've humiliated him.'

Sally sighed. 'Men and their pride.

His father's the same.'

She pursed her lips and her soft brown eyes were full of sympathy as Hedra struggled to fight her tears. 'I never meant to hurt him, Sally. Jem is the last person in the world I would hurt.'

Sally reached across to take Hedra's hand and give it a pat. 'Well, my lovely, you must find a way of telling him just that.'

Hedra left Gribble Farm feeling even more dispirited than ever. Instead of turning for home she struck out across the moor, heading for the cliff path. She needed space, time to clear her head.

But her head was full of pictures and they were all of Jem's angry face as he stalked off, leaving her on the hillside above the harbour last night. There was nothing she could say that would change his opinion of her. Head down she tramped on, knowing enough now to stay well back from the cliff edge.

Something on the edge of her vision brought her to a halt — a movement in the gorse. She held her breath, eyes glued to the spot where the bushes had moved. There it was again, not the wind, but something or someone was hiding there. A shiver of fear shot through her. This was the place that her frightened her before and sent her flying along the cliff path. But there was no Jem to come to her rescue today.

Stealing herself, she summoned her most commanding voice. 'I know you're there! Come out at once!'

There was a movement in the bush and Hedra forced herself to stand her ground as a figure, dark and stumbling, began to emerge. She concentrated on keeping her voice steady. 'Who are you?'

'Well, you've got the St Neot spunk, I'll say that for you.'

The familiar rasping voice made Hedra gasp. 'Uncle Edgar! We thought you'd drowned!' She kept her distance.

'Not afraid of your old uncle, are you?' he hissed, and his lip curled as he staggered towards her.

Hedra put a hand to her head. 'I don't understand,' she said. 'What are you doing here, hiding out on the moors?'

'I'm here to protect you, little niece, baby girl of my favourite brother.'

'Protect me? From what?'

'From him, of course — Jem Pentreath! I've seen you and him together, watched the two of you.'

Hedra's face flamed. Had Edgar really been watching them?

'I've come back to make sure he leaves you alone.' His voice was coarse, menacing. This man — even though he was her father's brother — had no feelings for his family. He wasn't here to help her, but Hedra was in no doubt that he meant to harm Jem. Well she wouldn't let him justify that by using her as an excuse.

'You don't have to worry about that any more, Uncle Edgar. Jem Pentreath and I are no longer friends, if truth be told.'

Edgar was beside her now and Hedra

was shocked by his ragged, unkempt appearance. 'Since when has a St Neot not been good enough for a Pentreath?' he roared. 'He'll pay for his insult to my family!' Edgar had a stick and he was beating about in the brush as he spoke.

'No, Uncle!' Hedra desperately tried to find the words to calm him. 'It was I who wronged him. He hasn't insulted our family. He respects us.'

'I saw no respect when he attacked my men, attacked me!'

'But you tried to steal their boats. The Mellin Cove men were only defending themselves.'

But Edgar wasn't listening. His eyes were wild but his voice was chillingly quiet. 'I know who they are,' he said. 'I know who all of them are.'

He turned and began stumbling off. Hedra shouted after him, tried to call him back, but it was useless. He seemed oblivious to her presence and she watched his shambling figure move across the moor, ignoring the trodden paths, still muttering his chilling threats

159

— and realised that her Uncle Edgar was mad! He was also very dangerous. She had to warn Jem and the others. There was no telling now what he was capable of. He had no care for his own safety. His mind was set on revenge.

A bank of storm clouds was building far out to sea. If the weather turned the boats would head for port. Then she spotted them, just one sail at first, then another. As she strained she could make out several double-masted vessels heading towards Mellin Cove. She raced across the cliff top, her feet scattering pebbles, sidestepping larger boulders as she reached the turning for the village. Sheets of rain were already enveloping the harbour, but there was no sign of the luggers. Panting to get her breath back she stood on the quay, shielding her eyes from the steady drizzle as she concentrated on the harbour entrance.

Jem and the others were out there, somewhere very close now. 'Please let them be safe,' she whispered into the gathering storm. Then she saw it, the shape of the first mast slicing through the murk, followed by another as she counted all the boats into harbour. Every one of them had returned. Her eyes searched for Jem, and then she spotted him on board the Sally P.

A little pulse of annoyance throbbed through her as she realised she'd been right; this was his way of telling her he wanted no more to do with the Bright Star, or perhaps even her. But none of that was important now; she had to warn him about Edgar.

She waited, impatient for him to secure his boat. Then he saw her and her heart lurched. Had that been a smile? Yes, he was smiling at her. 'I've been waiting for you,' she said.

Jem looked down at her with tender eyes. 'I hoped you might be.'

She wasn't sure what he meant. 'Does this mean you've forgiven me?'

He nodded. 'The sea gives you plenty of time to think. Oh, Hedra, I've been stupid. Of course you were trying to help the Prados. It's the kind of sweet, generous thing you would do.'

She hadn't expected this and her stomach did somersaults. 'Does this mean we are still . . . ' she hesitated and looked up at him through her wet eyelashes, ' . . . friends?'

He laughed. 'I was hoping we could be a bit more than that.'

Her hand flew to her mouth. The delight of the last few seconds had almost made her forget her mission. 'I've come to warn you,' she said breathlessly. 'Edgar is back and he's planning something awful. Oh, Jem. I think he might try to kill you. He's bitter and vicious, looking for revenge.'

'Does he have any men with him?' he asked.

'I didn't see anyone. He's been hiding up on the moors. Remember where you found me that day?' Jem nodded. 'Well, a little beyond that point. I was frightened by something I thought I saw and just ran. Today I saw it again, just a movement in the bushes.' Her chin rose defiantly at the memory

162

and Jem couldn't suppress a grin. 'But this time I didn't run. I stood my ground and challenged whoever was there to show himself.' Jem's eyebrows arched in admiration. 'It was Edgar.' Hedra shivered as the scene came back to her. 'Oh Jem, he was like a madman, desperate.'

Jem put his arms around her and brushed the wet curls from her face. 'Let's get you somewhere dry,' he said, leading her to the little wooden building the fishermen used to store their nets.

The rain pattered noisily on the cobbles outside, but Hedra imagined she could still hear her uncle's venomous threats. 'Edgar wants revenge. I think he means to kill you, Jem. You didn't see the look in his eyes. He's insane.'

Jem tilted her chin and his lips came down gently on hers. Hedra closed her eyes as the tenderness of the sensation swept over her.

'You must go home now, Hedra,' he said softly. 'We'll deal with this.'

'What can you do?'

Jem sighed. 'Probably nothing until he shows his hand. But I'll pass the word round, tell people to be on their guard.'

* * *

The path was slippery and she took her time. There was a lot to think about. Jem had forgiven her, even kissed her — and she felt like dancing. As the lights of Mellin Hall emerged from the mist, she realised she was soaked through and hurried past the yard, her thoughts on a hot bath before the fire in her bedchamber.

If she had wandered into the stable to check on Molly, as was her usual habit when she returned from an outing, she would have seen that her mare had a new companion. The handsome black stallion was in the adjoining stall being tended by the stable boy after its long journey.

But today Hedra went directly to her

room, calling for a maid to fill a bath for her. A full hour and a half had passed before she was bathed and dressed and of a sufficiently respectable state to present herself downstairs.

Like herself, Kit had believed Edgar to be dead, drowned in the sea after his attempt to steal the luggers. She had plenty of news to relate. But Kit wasn't alone in the parlour and both men rose to greet her as she entered. She gasped. 'Edward! What a surprise. I didn't know you were coming.'

'A pleasant surprise, I hope,' he said, smiling and coming towards her, his arms outstretched.

'Of course,' she said, allowing herself to be kissed on the cheek.

'You look flushed. Is there a reason?' Kit asked, eyeing her suspiciously.

'Edgar is alive.'

'What? How do you know?' Kit's voice was incredulous.

'I've spoken to him — out on the moors. He's alive.' She paused, considering her words, but there was no other way of describing her uncle. 'He's totally insane now,' she said.

Kit gave an embarrassed cough. 'I'm sorry, Edward. Hedra has this discomforting habit of blurting things out.' He stopped to give his sister an admonishing stare. 'No matter how delicate they are.'

'There was nothing delicate about Edgar when I saw him,' Hedra persisted. 'He's completely mad.'

'That's enough,' Kit said stiffly. 'Edward doesn't want to hear this.'

'I'm sure Edward already knows about our wicked uncle. It's not exactly a secret, Kit. But it's a bit more serious this time. He is threatening to kill people. He made threats against the Mellin Cove people.'

Edward let out a long low breath. 'You do live on the edge down here.'

'You'll have to excuse my sister, Edward. I'm afraid she exaggerates.'

'I wish it was an exaggeration,' Hedra said, 'I'm afraid it's all too true.'

Edward glanced from brother to

sister and saw their serious faces. 'Should we go down to the harbour, offer our support?' He shrugged. 'I feel we should be doing something.'

'Jem is taking care of things,' Hedra said. 'I think we'll leave it to him.' She saw Edward's jaw tighten. She'd forgotten about the confrontation between the two men when they last met at the harbour and wished she hadn't mentioned Jem's name.

'Hedra's right,' Kit said. 'We must leave this to the village. Our appearance might make the situation worse.'

'But he's your uncle,' Edward protested. 'If Hedra's right and he does turn up to cause mischief, wouldn't it be better if you were there to . . . well, I don't know . . . calm him down?'

Kit turned to his sister. 'What do you think?'

'I don't think we could calm him down. You didn't see him. I truly believe he's insane. We should stand back and let the Mellin Cove men handle this.'

The talk of Edgar had created an atmosphere amongst the three of them and the evening meal was conducted in an uneasy silence.

As they were preparing to rise from the table there was a loud knocking on the door. Voices were heard in the hall and Seth came through to report.

'Well, who is it, Seth?' Kit demanded.

'It's Jem Pentreath, sir. Asking for Miss Hedra.'

'Have him come through, please.'

Seconds later Jem appeared, his expression rigid when he spotted Edward. 'Forgive me,' he said. 'I didn't know you had company.' He gave an uneasy cough and looked around. 'It was Hedra I wanted a word with.'

'It's all right, Jem,' Kit assured him. Hedra has told us about Edgar. Has he turned up?'

'No. That's what I've come to say. There's no sign of him down at the harbour. I don't think he'll appear tonight.'

'You're taking the threat seriously

168

then?' Edward said, his lip curling.

'Hedra seemed to think the threat is real, and that's enough for us.' Jem smiled across at Hedra and she coloured.

Even from this distance she could see Edward bristle. The last thing she wanted was another confrontation here in Kit's house. She took Jem's arm and walked with him to the door. 'It was thoughtful of you to let us know.'

When they reached the front door, Jem unhooked Hedra's hand and stared down at her. 'Thoughtful of me . . . ?' he repeated her words.

'Please don't get annoyed again,' she pleaded. 'That was for their benefit — or at least, Edward's.'

'Why is Edward here again?' Jem's eyebrow was raised accusingly.

Hedra took a deep breath. 'He wants me to marry him.' She paused searching for the words. 'I think he's come for the answer.'

Jem pursed his lips and Hedra could see the muscle in his jaw tighten.

'I take it then that you will be leaving with him,' he said.

'Do you want me to marry Edward?' Jem shrugged. 'Your choice.'

'I'm giving that choice to you, Jem. Do you want me to marry Edward?'

But the sound of an explosion drowned out his reply, and Kit and Edward rushed from the parlour.

'What's happened?' Kit shouted.

They ran outside in time to see the ball of flame leap into the sky.

'It's the boats!' Jem yelled. 'He's blown up the boats!'

11

Jem didn't wait for the others to react. He tore down the hill without a backward glance. Hedra tried to follow him, but for a split second, she felt rooted to the spot. It was like her recurring dream, when no matter how frantically she ran to escape some terrible danger, she couldn't progress an inch. Kit rushing past brought her back to her senses.

'No time to saddle the horses,' he cried. 'We must get down there.'

Then all three of them were running, Hedra desperately trying to keep up with the men. But when they arrived, breathless, at the harbour there was no fire, no burning boats, only groups of people staring mournfully out into the black water. Jem had arrived just ahead of them and he appeared as mystified as they were.

Then Hedra spotted Catherine Prado pushing her way through the gathering. Hedra put out a hand to draw her into their group. 'Whatever's happened, Catherine?'

The woman carried a lamp and Hedra could see that her normally ashen face was even more drawn. 'It's your uncle, Miss.' Her sympathetic glance flickered around the group, her eyes resting on Hedra. 'He's blown himself up, Miss,' she said.

Hedra clamped a hand over her mouth and stared from Catherine into the dark harbour.

'Can you tell us what's happened, Catherine?' Jem asked gently.

'He came running onto the harbour, banging on doors, rousing everyone, yelling that he would blow up the harbour and all of us with it. He was brandishing a bundle of explosives. No one could get near him.' Her face crumpled and jerky sobs shook her thin body.

She met Hedra's eyes and nodded.

'Your uncle, Miss, he ran to the boats and climbed onto the Sally P.' She slid a brief glance towards Jem. 'We could all see him out there, waving his arms and ranting that the fishermen had to pay. Then there was an almighty bang that shook the whole harbour . . . a flash of white light . . . ' She shuddered, shaking her head. 'It was like the whole world was exploding and then nothing — and Edgar had gone.'

Kit was first to speak. 'His body must be recovered,' he said, then turning to Jem, 'Is there a boat I can use?'

'Follow me,' Jem said. 'I'll go with you.'

'Are you all right, Hedra?' Edward was by her side. She'd forgotten he was there. 'I'll take you back to Mellin Hall.'

'No,' she said fiercely. 'I'll wait for Jem and Kit to get back.'

Edward kept his voice low. 'I don't think that's a good idea.'

Catherine touched her arm. 'The gentleman's right, Miss, you should go home. Leave it to the men now. There's nothing more we can do here.'

Edward took off his jacket and draped it around Hedra's shoulders and she allowed herself to be led back up the winding path to Mellin Hall. Hot drinks were prepared and Hedra paced the floor until the sound of cart wheels could be heard rumbling up the drive.

She made to run to the door, but Edward stopped her. 'We should stay here,' he said gently. 'Until Kit comes in.'

She waited, eyes glued to the door until Jem arrived with her brother. She could tell by their grim expressions that their task had not been easy.

'We've brought Edgar back,' Kit said wearily. 'I'll send a message to Penmere. Father will have to be told.'

Hedra bit her lip. Despite Edgar's past behaviour, he was still a St Neot, and the family would do right by him.

The journey home would be difficult and Hedra was not looking forward to it, but she didn't know if that was because of any sadness she felt at her

174

uncle's death. He had certainly been a rogue, but he was still family. She suspected her gloomy mood was more to do with leaving Mellin Hall — and Jem. They'd seemed closer these last few days, but perhaps she had only imagined that he had been on the point of declaring his feelings, of telling her he loved her.

Even if she had no future with Jem, she knew she could never marry Edward. When she told him, he'd taken her decision with the courtesy she had expected of him. He'd kissed her hand and wished her happiness. A little pang of guilt twitched in her heart as she watched him ride out of the yard, but she couldn't make herself love him.

Hedra and Kit's journey began an hour later as they cantered behind the carriage bearing their uncle back to Penmere.

'There's a rider coming,' Kit said, shielding his eyes to squint into the early morning sun. 'I think it's Jem.'

Hedra's heart skipped a beat at the

mention of his name. They pulled up their horses to wait for him.

He arrived at a gallop, a little breathless. 'Would it be in order for me to join you? It's true Edgar had no love for me, nor I for him.' He paused, then added, 'But I hope the rest of the St Neot family consider me a friend.'

Hedra looked to her brother for the answer and Kit smiled and extended his hand. 'You're welcome to join us, Jem,' he said.

They spoke little on the journey, but Hedra's heart was soaring. The task ahead was solemn, but her mood of gloom had vanished. The late February sun was shining and Jem was riding by her side. He would meet her father and the rest of her family. Deep inside her, a little knot of excitement was growing. As they neared Penmere, their eyes met and they shared a secret smile as they rode past the spot where Jem had hidden from Edgar's men that night, where he had held her safe until the danger had passed.

As they approached the manor house, Hedra saw the great oak door open and she threw herself from her mare and rushed forward to hug her father and brother. 'I'm so glad to be home,' she whispered.

Both men stared at the carriage that bore Edgar's body. Then Matthew issued instructions where to take him. Only then did their questioning gazes turn to Jem. Hedra held back to allow Kit to introduce him. 'This is a good friend from Mellin Cove, Father. He's come to pay his respects.

Jem dismounted, but his look told Hedra he felt a little uncomfortable. He extended his hand to her father. 'Jem Pentreath, sir,' he said.

Matthew St Neot took his hand and nodded. 'Welcome to Penmere, Mr Pentreath. Friends are always welcome here.'

Jem visibly relaxed and Hedra beamed at him as they followed her father into the house.

Family meals at Penmere were never

formal and, despite the solemn nature of the occasion, there was laughter and happy faces round the table that evening. No one questioned the simple clothes Jem wore, his work-rough hands, or his weather-beaten appearance. Only later, when the family had dispersed around the room, did Matthew broach the subject.

'I've met your young man's father. Isn't he a farmer?'

Hedra's eyes rounded as she stared at her father. Matthew patted her hand and re-filled his pipe. 'Don't look so surprised, girl,' he said, amusement in his voice. 'It's obvious there's something between you two.'

Hedra felt the colour creep up her neck as she glanced across at Jem, who was deep in conversation with Nathan and looking very much at home.

'We're friends, Father, like Kit said . . .'

Matthew smiled and slid his spectacles further down his nose to consider his daughter. 'If you say so, my dear,' he said. 'If you say so.'

The church next morning was surprisingly crowded. Hedra imagined most mourners had come, like Jem, out of respect for her family and she hoped her father took comfort from that. Looking around the faces in the stark wooden pews she suspected he was the only one present who felt real sadness at Edgar's death.

'You didn't know him as a boy,' he'd told her the previous evening. 'He was kind then, full of life . . . but that was before the bitterness took over.' His eyes had hooded and Hedra reached out to him when he said, 'I lost my brother a very long time ago — but that's the Edgar I will remember.'

A tear trickled down her cheek and she had whisked it away. Then she felt Jem's hand on her shoulder. He leaned forward and whispered in her ear, 'Are you all right, Hedra?'

The concern in his voice made her turn. She had looked into his eyes, and the wave of tenderness that swept over her made her weak.

If her father had asked then if she loved this man, she would reply 'With all my heart.' But Matthew had no need to ask. He had glanced across and seen the look that passed between this stranger and his daughter.

Few tears were shed for Edgar St Neot, and those that were had probably been from sentiment rather than genuine sorrow, but it was right that he should be interred in Penmere Church-yard, beside his ancestors. In his life he had brought so much trouble to the people of Mellin Cove. He would certainly have killed Jem, if he could. Now that they were free of him, Hedra was beginning to experience the same release she imagined the others felt. She and Jem could return there, and she could hold her head high again.

The relief following the solemnity of the church service was evident around the table as the family dined that evening. Baby Conan had joined the group and lay gurgling happily in his cradle by Rachel's side as the meal progressed. Jem's eyes seldom left Hedra's face and she radiated a contentment she had never known before.

After the meal, Matthew called Jem aside and Hedra felt a flutter of unease as she watched them walk out into the garden. She tried to imagine all the reasons her father would have for talking with Jem. He'd mentioned he knew Jem's father — would they be sharing memories? She didn't think so. They were talking about her. In her father's eyes, no man would ever be good enough for his daughter. But if she had to marry, then he might accept someone like Edward, someone with breeding, education and wealth.

Her heart began to sink as she watched the door to the garden, waiting for them to return. It felt like forever before they reappeared. Hedra studied their faces, but she could detect no anger, no sign of harsh words, no evidence of any disagreement. She stood up and moved towards them, her expression questioning.

'I think you two have things to discuss,' her father said, indicating that they should go into his study. Hedra looked from one to the other and a strange feeling was beginning to stir inside her. Jem took her arm and propelled her gently into the small, book-lined room, then he closed the door. She waited, not daring even to breathe. He took her hand and she looked into his eyes — and suddenly she knew what he was going to say.

When the words came she tried to retain her composure, behave in the restrained fashion gentlemen of her class expect when they propose to a lady. But this was her and Jem, and when the words came she threw her arms round his neck and cried, 'Yes, yes, yes!'

★ ★ ★

It was some time before they joined the others, and Hedra's heart was still beating out of control as she and Jem shared their news. There were hugs, and tears and glasses clinking as everyone crowded round to offer their congratulations. Hedra's hand was in Jem's, and they were surrounded by the people she loved most in the world. She had never been so happy.

'When is the wedding to be?' Rachel asked, slipping an arm around her sister-in-law's waist. Hedra looked at Jem.

'Soon,' he grinned happily. 'But there are some things I must do first.'

'Secrets already?' Hedra teased.

'Call it a surprise,' he replied.

'You should fix a date, you know. Many arrangements have to be made,' Rachel advised. 'The wedding has to be held at Penmere of course, that goes without saying. Then there will be fittings for the bridal gown, flowers, guest lists, a banquet to arrange . . . ' She went on in full swing.

A tiny black cloud was beginning to settle over Hedra. More than anything in the world she wanted to marry Jem, but until now she had just never considered the actual wedding.

How could she think of leaving Mellin Cove — leaving Jem — even if only for a short time while the arrangements were attended to? And what of Jem's family, and all the others at Mellin Cove? They could hardly be expected to travel to Penmere, yet it would be unthinkable not to have them at the wedding.

The solution was simple. She and Jem would be married at Mellin Hall.

'But you can't!' Rachel exclaimed, when Hedra announced her intention. 'What about all the arrangements?'

'We can still do all those, but at Mellin,' Hedra said.

Rachel screwed her face up. 'But it's so far away.'

'Which means we will have to be extremely well organised.' Hedra smiled sweetly at her sister-in-law.

184

Nathan joined them and put an arm round his wife's shoulder. 'It's Hedra and Jem's wedding,' he reminded her gently. 'It's for them to decide where it will be held.'

Rachel had never visited Mellin Hall and envisaged a cold, inhospitable granite building, perched high on the wild Cornish moors. It wasn't her idea of the ideal wedding venue.

'I have a proposal,' said Hedra. 'Why don't you all come to stay for a few days — weeks even — the whole family, baby Conan included. That way you can familiarise yourself with the house and meet Jem's family and all our friends. Then, once you know what the setting is like,' Hedra was getting into her stride now, 'we can start making the arrangements from there.'

Rachel was still a little unsure, but Hedra could tell she was already considering the possibilities.

Kit joined the group and Hedra said, 'Tell Rachel how lovely it is at Mellin. I'm trying to convert her to the idea of holding our wedding there.'

'Come and see for yourself, Rachel.' He waved a hand to include everyone in the room. 'Why don't you all come?' he smiled at Rachel. 'Then we could really celebrate my sister's betrothal to my best friend.' He laid a hand on Jem's shoulder.

★   ★   ★

And so it was agreed. The four St Neots, with Bessie, Jonas and Ellen, the kitchen maid following behind on a wagon, travelled to Mellin Hall the following week. February had slid unnoticed into March and the first stirrings of spring were in the air. Several more village women were taken on to help prepare food and spruce up the Hall until it shone like a new pin.

'Well, Rachel,' Hedra asked, as the first lambs began to bleat at Gribble Farm, 'what do you think of Mellin?'

They had returned from a walk on the moors, with baby Conan secure in a specially made sling, held snugly against Rachel's chest.

'It's a bracing enough location and not unpleasing,' she conceded, 'but there are arrangements that can only be made in Penmere, and we will have to visit shops in Penzance, perhaps even Truro, to find the silks and brocades for your gown.'

'No need,' Hedra smiled, holding up a hand to silence further discussion. 'My bridal gown will be made here in Mellin.'

Rachel looked askance. 'You have seamstresses here in this place who are sufficiently skilled?' her voice rose in disbelief.

Hedra nodded. 'Jem's mother, Sally, has offered to make my wedding gown and I have accepted.'

'Tell me this isn't true.' Rachel's hand fluttered at her throat.

But Hedra threw her arms around her and danced her round the room.

'Please be happy for me, Rachel. I want the most blissful day of my life to take place here at Mellin, surrounded by the people I love. I don't care about fine silks and wedding gowns made by the finest seamstresses in Truro. But I do care about my family and all our friends, and I want everyone here to see Jem and I wed. The ceremony will be simple, held here in the village church, but we'll have a feast of delicious food, plenty of wine and lots of dancing.' She drew back to gauge Rachel's reaction. 'Will you give me a wedding day like that, Rachel?'

Her sister-in-law's expression softened and she held her arms wide to Hedra. 'You're an impossible girl,' she said laughing, 'I hope your Jem knows what he is taking on.'

★ ★ ★

The wedding day was drawing near and Hedra had gasped in admiration at the exquisite bridal gown Sally created from the bolt of fine silk that Rachel had arranged to be sent from Truro, and a set of rooms was being prepared at the Hall in readiness for the newly weds to take up residence.

But when Jem saw them he pursed his lips. 'Very nice,' he said following Hedra's conducted tour. 'But you do realise that these rooms will only be temporary accommodation, don't you?'

'What's wrong with them?' She frowned. 'I know they're not ideal, but I thought they would suffice until we can manage a place of our own.'

Jem took her hand and propelled her out the door. 'I have something to show you,' he grinned, 'but it's out on the moor.'

At first Hedra thought he was leading her to Gribble Farm, but he turned onto an unfamiliar path and stopped at a ruined cottage. From here the slated roof of Mellin Hall was just visible to her right, and if she stood on tiptoe, she could just see Gribble Farm nestling amongst its little network of fields below.

'This is where we will live, Hedra,' he said. 'Right here on this spot.'

'But it's a ruin!'

'It is now, but in a few weeks' time, this cottage will be rebuilt to twice its original size. It will be our wedding gift from the men of the village,' he said, hugging her. 'Of course,' he added with a teasing smile, 'we will be adding extra bits over the years . . . as our family expands . . . '

'How many extra bits do you think we will need?' she laughed.

Jem held her close and she could feel the whisper of his breath in her hair. 'Quite a few,' he murmured.

They turned to look out at the wide expanse of clear ocean.

Jem's voice was husky as he told her, 'On summer evenings the sun sinks into the horizon and turns the sky crimson.' He laid his cheek against her hair as they watched a herring gull soar effortlessly above the moving sea. 'This will be our home, Hedra.'

And her heart was bursting with love and contentment as she whispered back, 'It's just perfect.'

We do hope that you have enjoyed reading this large print book.

Did you know that all of our titles are available for purchase?

We publish a wide range of high quality large print books including:
Romances, Mysteries, Classics
General Fiction
Non Fiction and Westerns

Special interest titles available in large print are:
The Little Oxford Dictionary
Music Book, Song Book
Hymn Book, Service Book

Also available from us courtesy of Oxford University Press:
Young Readers' Dictionary
(large print edition)
Young Readers' Thesaurus
(large print edition)

For further information or a free brochure, please contact us at:
Ulverscroft Large Print Books Ltd.,
The Green, Bradgate Road, Anstey,
Leicester, LE7 7FU, England.
Tel: (00 44) **0116 236 4325**
Fax: (00 44) **0116 234 0205**

In hospital, Alison Montgomery cannot remember her own name. She hears the doctors' hushed whispers — sees their worried glances, which speak of the dark secrets lying just beyond the locked shutters of her memory. Then they bring her the stranger who says he's her husband. But why can't she remember loving a man as compelling as Nicholas Montgomery? And yet the shadows in his eyes clearly reveal that there's something in their past better left forgotten . . .

SECRETS IN THE SAND

Jane Retallick

When Sarah Daniels moves to a sleepy Cornish village her neighbour, local handyman and champion surfer, Ben Trelawny is intrigued. He falls in love with her stunning looks and quirky ways — but who is this woman? Why does she lock herself in her cottage — and why she is so guarded? When Ben finally gets past Sarah's barriers, a national newspaper reporter arrives in the village. Sarah disappears, making a decision that puts her life and future in jeopardy.

WITHOUT A SHADOW OF DOUBT

Teresa Ashby

Margaret Harris's boss, Jack Stanton, disappears in suspicious circumstances. The police want to track him down, but Margaret believes in him and wants to help him prove his innocence. Meanwhile, Bill Colbourne wants to marry her, but, unsure of her feelings, she can't think of the future until she finds Jack. And, when she does meet with him in Spain, she finally has to admit to Bill that she can't marry him — it's Jack Stanton who she loves.